THIS IS NOT THE END

Stories by
Peter Raposo

APS Books
Yorkshire

APS Books,
The Stables Field Lane,
Aberford,
West Yorkshire,
LS25 3AE

APS Books is a subsidiary of the APS Publications imprint

www.andrewsparke.com

First published worldwide by APS Books in 2022

A catalogue record for this book is available from the British Library

CONTENTS

1. BEFORE THE APOCALYPSE

The Suicide Club   3

Remembering Brandon Lee   18

Searching For Kenzaburo Oe   19

The Life Of A Novelist   28

The Typewriter   43

Doors That Lead Nowhere   45

Friday 3rd May 2013   48

The Spoiled One   50

Inebriated Brain   56

The Poet And Me   58

Lost & Found (& Left Behind)   64

Nothing Left   65

Jerusalem   66

The Jealous One   67

What I Saw   76

Too Good   78

A Portrait Of The End   80

The End   82

17 Year Old Poet   84

2. AFTER THE APOCALYPSE

This Is Not The End   87

Underground   118

The Tramp's Tale   131

The End   133

The First Book   135

1 - BEFORE THE APOCALYPSE

THE SUICIDE CLUB

It started like some kind of plague, an epidemic, some sort of disaster, a virus, a fashion (for some), a deadly fashion, a desperate act, the last act (for some), and something like that was unheard of. Around the world, in places like Tokyo, Osaka, Texas, Marseille, Toronto, Lisbon, and even Beijing, forty five teenagers killed themselves on the same day, probably at the same time, too, leaving behind no notes, no clues whatsoever for their suicides. None of the teenagers died alone. They were all in groups of two, three and even four, and at first no one could explain what made them do this; this collective suicide, but then rumours started to be spread online, around campuses, bars, male bathrooms, female bathrooms, everywhere; rumours about suicide clubs, suicide holidays, suicide for the needy, and that's when the world found out that there existed a any number of online suicide clubs where people could chat and give advice to others on how to choose the best way to reave themselves of their lives. And a person didn't even have to die alone. You could arrange to meet up with others and commit collective suicide. One of those websites was called *alt.suicide.holiday*, or "ash" if you couldn't be bothered to say the whole name, and the members of this virtual community called themselves "Ashers", and there you could find good tips on how to poison yourself with carbon monoxide. Definitely not a site for happy people. Then again, it was also the wrong site for depressed people.

With time, due to pressure from the government and mostly from people who lost beloved ones to suicide, some of those suicide clubs were closed or abolished, but, nonetheless, collective suicide was still happening throughout the world. There was also the case of Hiroshi Maeue who proposed to someone online that they kill themselves together, and then he tied the person with ropes in a car, in this case a woman, and choked her to death. Two other victims, a 21-year-old college student and a 14-year-old high school student, were similarly dispatched by this monster, Hiroshi. On July 28th, 2009, Hiroshi was hanged in Osaka. Four years and a few months later my brother Lester committed suicide alongside three other strangers. That's when I found out about the BogMan.

I already knew that Lester was suffering from depression but I didn't know that it was that bad. Or maybe I was too busy with my own life to even care for my younger brother. Yes, I guess that's what happened.

Even as a child Lester was usually in a depressive mood, always talking about death and going to the Other Side, and he hated the world and his life -and the suffering of so many people around him. Once, by accident, he stepped on a snail outside our house and then burst into tears. By the time he was 19-years-old, just before he went to university, he was already on medication; Prozac and other shit, going through life looking like a zombie. I guess our parents were in some part to blame for that, because, while they gave me a lot of their love and time, by the time they had Lester they were too tired to give him anything apart from grief, and even as a baby, when he cried for milk, our mother would sigh deeply and curse before, reluctantly, seeing to Lester's needs. I was ten-years-old by the time Lester was born, and the reason why there's such a big gap between us both is because our parents didn't want to have a second child. Lester was an "accident", and our parents hated "accidents".

Because of that big age gap between us I didn't have a lot to do with my brother, and by the time I was twenty (and my brother was ten) I was already living away from home.

Our worlds were different but I'd like to think that I loved him.

I'm sure I loved him, didn't I?

Did I really?

Did I love him enough?

And if I did how come I wasn't there for him when he needed me?

My parents didn't have a lot to do with Lester's upbringing. They simply hired a couple of nannies to look after him, and that was it. Everything he learned, he learnt it from his nannies, not from our parents.

On the last talk we had over the phone, I remember him saying, "Our parents gave you all the love they had and I was left with nothing."

That was such a terrible thing to say –but it was true- and I didn't know what to say apart from a feeble, "I'm sorry."

"It's not your fault," Lester said and afterwards he said he had to go.

On the next day I got a call from our mother saying that Lester was dead.

When I heard her saying that he was gone to the Other Side, my heart seemed to freeze temporarily and I found it hard to breathe. For a brief moment I thought I was going to drop dead too. Over the phone mother told me what happened and how Lester's body was found in a car along with three other people.

"The police said it was collective suicide," she said. And then she said something else, and something else after that, more words coming out of her mouth but I was too confused to say a thing.

I remembered my brother's last call to me, his soft voice on the phone, and then I saw him as a child, always sitting alone in a corner, watching TV alone, reading alone, studying alone, going through life always alone, without anyone to guide him, to love him. Only in death did he have someone with him.

"Are you there?" my mother asked and I said, "Yes."

"Are you feeling alright? I didn't think the two of you were that close," she said, and I detected nothing in her speech, not a hint of sadness, nothing at all…nothing.

Poor Lester, I failed you too, my little brother.

I put the phone down and I lit a cigarette. Mother called me back and asked, "What the hell was that for?"

"How do you feel, mother?" I asked and took a long drag from my cigarette. "How do you feel now that Lester's gone? Do you even miss him?"

Smoke came out of my mouth and dissolved in the air, like ashes, like hope, like the dreams of my little brother. Like nothing. Like the emptiness of our souls.

My questions were followed by a long silence, and while I waited for mother to say something, I scanned the room where I was, my small living room, a room surrounded with expensive technology, large shelves filled with books, DVDs and CDs that went up to the ceiling, a couple of plants that needed to be watered, and I felt suffocated in that room, so I put the phone down for the second time and I went out. Before I left the apartment I grabbed my coat, my mobile phone, a small notebook and a pen, my pack of cigarettes, a few coins that were lying around, and then I went out for a walk.

For the next forty minutes or so it looked as if I was walking without direction, and the buildings around me looked so ugly, like gigantic stone monsters that were coming back to life, while the faces of the people that walked past me looked distorted.

A mother and a daughter walked past me, and, accidentally, I brushed against the woman without even noticing it, and the woman turned to me and said, "Weirdo."

I looked at her, and then at her daughter, and the little girl stuck her tongue out, aiming it at me with venom. The child was ugly, as ugly as her mother, and I wanted to say something back, at least apologise for having bumped into the woman, but they gave me their backs and kept on walking. Then, seconds later, while I was still looking at the mother and daughter, a young man came running out of a shopping mall, holding in his hands a lady's bag and a mobile phone, and he was being pursued by a fat security guard and a woman wearing a white blouse and a short blue skirt, both of them shouting, "Stop! Stop!" and when the woman tried to come down the steps, one of the heels of her shoes broke, she slipped over, and then rolled all the way down, like a scene of a movie, and those of us who witnessed it all saw her as she tumbled down and rolled and screamed, and the fat security guard chased the thief, not stopping to help the woman because he had a job to do. The woman's legs were covered in blood and someone came over to help her, and then more people started to come out of the shopping mall, not to help the woman but to see what was happening, and we all saw the security guard run slowly up the road while the young criminal was almost out of sight, and then the security guard stopped, his hands resting on his knees as he looked down, and then he stood straight just before he collapsed on the ground. So now there was a woman bleeding on the floor and a security guard lying on the floor, probably hit by a stroke, all of this happening on the day that I heard my brother had died.

I heard sirens not that far from where I was, followed by shots, and I kept on walking. Up the road I went, and I walked past the security guard, his face by now pale, death-like, and I saw someone applying first aid to him but he wasn't moving, and a few metres ahead I saw the police standing around a body, blood on the floor, blood running slowly along the dirty pavement, and I saw a woman's bag on the floor; its contents lying on the floor; lipstick, a small box of tissues, coins, a pocket watch, and as I was staring at it, a cop put his arm around me and told me to move on because there was nothing there to see, and when he said that I looked him in the eye and said, "Right," which was the wrong thing to say.

Another cop came to see what was happening but I kept on walking while both cops kept staring at me.

I walked past an old building where I used to work many years ago; its glass front door had been smashed by vandals or drunks or someone else (a junkie? an old employee?), and I saw a man inside the building shouting at a woman. I couldn't hear what he was saying but I saw his mouth wide open, his face as red as a tomato, and he was waving his hands in front of the woman, looking as if he was ready to punch her. The woman had her head down and she looked as if she could burst into tears at any moment. I lit another cigarette and I stood there, in front of the glass door, staring at the woman and the man. He was wearing a black suit and a white shirt, the last two buttons undone, and she had on a black skirt, a few inches just over the knees, a white shirt too, and a black cardigan. The man's mouth then stopped moving and he stamped his right foot on the floor before walking away. And even after he was gone the woman just stood there, head down, and she looked as if she was waiting for the floor to come alive and swallow her. She stood there for a few minutes, just staring at the floor, shoulders hunched forward, and no one said a word to her. I was about to reach the end of the cigarette when she finally looked up, and then she looked at me. And she looked sad, really sad. And I walked away.

I walked all the way towards the house where my brother used to live, some place downtown where a lot of artists and junkies or a mixture of both lived. A female transgender walked past me and said *hi*. I said *hi* too. A young woman was sitting on a crate, a typewriter in front of her, and she was chanting something in Hebrew. She nodded and I nodded back.

I pressed the doorbell and I waited. Seconds later a thin, old woman opened the front door for me, and when she saw me she smiled, and afterwards she hugged me. I just stood there, cold as a rock, taking it all in. The woman, who happened to be the landlady, said, "I'm sorry." Then she said, "I'm so sorry." And afterwards she said a lot of other stuff but I was too numb to pay attention to what she was saying.

Finally, to my relief, she stopped talking, but then she stared at me for a few seconds, and it looked like she could see right through me, see what a fake I was, a cold and cruel and cynical man, and I felt scared; I felt like crying, but only briefly. Mistaking confusion for sadness, she took my hand and led me into my brother's room. She opened the door and left me there on my own.

I stood there for a few seconds, outside the room, scanning the inside of the room with tired eyes. Strangely enough, seeing how much I had walked just to get there, I felt as if I shouldn't go inside the room. As weird as it may sound, I even think I heard a voice inside me saying, "Keep away. There's evil here. Keep away."

I took a step forward. And another. And another. And...

The place was spotless, a contrast to my place I might add; Lester had always been a very tidy person, with books neatly piled on a desk, records (vinyl) stacked properly and neatly inside a square plastic box, magazines in Muji boxes, etc. His large bedroom was a contrast to my messy apartment.

There were no pictures of him lying around or any pictures of any of us; me, mum, dad, a girlfriend, a boyfriend, a friend, nothing. It was almost as if Lester had no one, and that, sadly, had probably been the case. As I stood there in the middle of the room, surrounded by his things, I suddenly realised that I didn't even know his date of birth. We were strangers in every sense of the way, related only by blood. I scanned the titles of every single book he had as I tried to search for answers, for some kind of clues, but answers for what and what kind of clues?

Lester had been lonely and we all had failed him. What else did I need to know?

Most of his books had depressing tittles or were depressing or looked depressed, and I had read none of them. Or most of them.

The books were:

Jay Asher – *Thirteen Reasons Why*
Socrates Adams – *Everything's Fine*
Anonymous – *Go Ask Alice*
Tao Lin – *Eeeee Eee Eeee*
Tao Lin – *Bed*
Tao Lin – *Shoplifting from American Apparel*
Michael Thomas Ford – *Suicide Notes*
Erlend Loe – *Naïve. Super*

Joanna Kenrick – *Red Tears*
Sam Pink – *Person*
Noah Cicero – *The Human War*
Noah Cicero – *Best Behaviour*
Caroline Kettlewell – *Skin Game*
Howard Buten – *When I was five I killed myself*
Patricia McCormick – *Cut*
Peter Wild – *The Passenger*
Melissa P. – *The Scent of your Breath*
Elizabeth Wurtzel – *Prozac Nation*
Sylvia Plath – *The Bell Jar*
Rick Springfield – *Late, Late at Night*
John Green – *The Fault in Our Stars*
Andrew Kaufman – *The Waterproof Bible*
Ben Lerner – *Leaving the Atocha Station*
Edwidge Danticat – *Breath, Eyes, Memory*
Blake Butler – *Scorch Atlas*
Knut Hamsun – *Hunger*
Henry Miller – *Black Spring*
Henry Miller – *Tropic of Cancer*
Henry Miller – *Tropic of Capricorn*

I only knew the books by Miller, Hamsun and Plath.

"Who was this stranger?" I wondered. I touched the spines of the books as my eyes surveyed every title. "Who was this strange man that read these strange books?"

I opened a drawer and saw socks and underwear; normal socks and plain underwear, nothing kinky or strange. I opened another drawer and saw t-shirts, long sleeves, short sleeves, all plain and dull, lifeless, just like Lester. I searched around the room for something but what? What was I looking for?

Redemption?

Forgiveness?

An excuse for my coldness towards my own brother?

All of it?

There was nothing under his bed, nothing under the pillows, nothing (but clothes) in the small wardrobe.

I searched in his desk for something, anything that could explain to me why; why did he do it. But isn't loneliness and despair reason enough for someone to commit suicide?

There were notepads filled with poems, some written by Lester, others copied from other poetry books. I remembered once seeing Lester's name in a magazine over a poem of his. Back then I barely paid attention to his name, never mind his poetry. To us all, to the family, he was invisible. He might as well be dead if that was the case.

Poor Lester, how many nights did you spend alone, crying while we were enjoying ourselves? How many nights did you cry injustice to the world, cried for lack of love, wondered why you weren't loved?

Sorry little brother. I'm so sorry now, now that is too late, too late to bring you back, and even if we could bring you back who's to say we wouldn't do the same thing again?

I searched through his drawers, through the pages of his books, and then something fell out of *The Bell Jar*. It was a little leaflet, a round leaflet, shaped like a circle. In one side there was a sad face, and on the other side there was the line: *Don't die alone. see the BogMan.*

Underneath that sentence was a web link.

I left his place without bothering to say a word to his landlady and I made my way to the nearest internet café. The sky was dark then with the promise of rain not far behind. A bus packed with tourists was parked outside the net café I was heading to, and when I looked at the faces inside it, I saw a sad girl with her face pressed against the window. She looked like she was lost in her own world, lost in oblivion, walking along a road that would take her nowhere. There was a woman sitting beside her, a woman that —face wise- looked like the girl; she must have been the girl's mother, and while the woman was laughing with someone else, the young girl's face remained miserable.

The suffering can be there, right in front of our eyes, and we still fail to see it, either because we don't care or because we're too busy with other matters.

I made my way inside the café, walked to the counter, ordered a cappuccino, and paid for my drink and for thirty minutes online. The place wasn't that busy; there were two people sitting at a table, chatting and drinking coffee, and there were three other people using the computers. I sat next to a Japanese girl and I entered the pin number that I had been given at the counter. Once I was online, I typed the BogMan's website address only to discover that it had been closed down.

I didn't let that put me off and I wrote BogMan and moved the arrow towards the search button before pressing it. The chase was on.

For the next twenty five minutes or so I entered the world of suicide, a world filled with cries for help, sad tales, stories of abandonment, self-inflicted pain, cuts, rape, physical abuse, verbal abuse, and there were thousands of people on dozens of forums with sad tales to tell, but I wasn't really interested in their tales. I just wanted to find out who the BogMan was, but time was running out, and unless I paid to use the computer for a bit longer, soon it would switch off by itself. I logged off. I could always use it at home for as long as I wanted. My cappuccino was untouched. I massaged the area above my eyes gently and then I closed them briefly. Then a voice beside me said, "You won't find the BogMan online."

I opened my eyes and looked to my right. The young Japanese girl sitting beside me was staring at me, her eyes so needy and so sad. For some reasons she reminded me of Lester. In a way she was as much as a stranger to me as he was. How sad was that?

We left the café and went to a park nearby where we could smoke and talk in peace without anyone listening to us. We lit our first cigarettes just outside the café and I took a good look at the young girl standing beside me. She was quite short. Thin, too. Not a stunner but not ugly either. She wore flat shoes, thin-fitted jeans, a plain white blouse and a thin black cardigan. Nothing about her was extravagant or said, "Look at me!"

Even the book she was reading, *The Apartment* by Greg Baxter, appeared quite normal.

I wanted to ask her name but instead I just nodded when she asked me if I wanted to go to the park for a chat.

We walked in silence, past fruit stalls, record stalls, book stalls, stalls filled with junk, little bars and cafés, past an old Chinese takeaway where I went once or twice a week, and then we got to the park.

We kept on walking, the little Japanese girl walking a few steps ahead of me, leading the way, and then we sat under a tree. The sky was still grey and the rain was still promising to come out but maybe that promise would stay unfulfilled.

Four young men were playing with a frisbee while another one, a bit chubbier than the other four, sat on the grass on his own with a book by Aleksandar Hemon for company.

The Japanese girl saw me staring at him and said, "There's always one who is left out, the outsider of the group, the one who doesn't belong, the one who is sad."

I looked at her and she was staring at the young man, maybe even past the young man: maybe she was already staring at the end. The air was getting colder so she buttoned her cardigan right to the top. Up in the trees, the squirrels and the birds stared at us and at every single person walking past.

The Japanese girl said, "One day these poor animals won't have a place to live. Already their habitat is being restricted. Only God knows what will happen in the near future."

Just being there for a small amount of time, staring at her bland face and sad eyes, listening to her morbid talk, made me feel depressed too.

I said, "The BogMan. Tell me more about him."

"How do you know that it's a he?" she asked.

"I assumed it's a he because it says BogMan. If it was a woman it would say BogWoman," I said.

"You're funny," she said, her face remaining as bland as before.

Yeah, fucking hilarious.

"The BogMan leaves leaflets in bookshops, libraries, cafés, toilet cubicles, in places where he knows that people who need help will read them. Most of it is word of mouth," she said.

"Has anyone ever seen this BogMan?" I asked.

"Yes. I heard that once a group of four is gathered, ready to depart this world, the BogMan comes to see them."

"What's your name?"

"I'm Asa."

"I'm Karl. Karl with a K."

"As in Karl Marx?"

"Yes."

"So tell me, Karl with a K, do you want to meet the BogMan?"

Lester's funeral was as morbid as his life, a showcase for emptiness and coldness. There were four people present; me, mother, and two friends of his. Father couldn't make it to the funeral. He was in Dubai taking care of some businesses. Those things had always been more important to him than Lester.

Once Lester's body was buried, his two friends came over to shake our hands and give their condolences. No one shed a tear for Lester, not even his friends, certainly not me. Our hearts were cold and dead, working only when we were staring at a small screen in front of our eyes, sharing our life online with others via pictures, silly messages or tweets.

I wanted to speak with mother about Lester, find out more about the brother who had been a stranger to me all of my life, but she said she was in a rush, short for time (aren't we all nowadays in this chaotic society?), because she had an interview to give to a magazine.

"This will help me sell more copies of my new book. God knows I need any free publicity I can get," she said.

"But you just buried your son!" I said, shocked by her behaviour. But why was I shocked seeing that she had always been like this?

"Nothing sells more than a sad story," she said, and then hurried back to her Mercedes.

I lit a cigarette.

I looked around.

Two skinny pigeons were staring at me, probably wondering where all the food was. "No food in here unless you're an earthworm," I thought.

In that place of death the past was digested by the present, the present was only seconds away from becoming the past, and the fat worms were waiting on our flesh.

A small creature came running from behind a tree. At first I thought it was a squirrel, only to realise that it was a rat as it ran past me. A big, fucking, disgusting rat.

My phone was ringing and I picked it up. I had a message from Asa. It said, *behind you*.

I turned around and I saw her on the other side, standing behind the gate, waving shyly at me. The cemetery looked empty as I made my way towards her. But then I saw a man eating biscuits inside the shed, and I saw someone else leaning against the same shed while having a cigarette, and I even think that I saw a woman dressed entirely in white disappear behind the shed.

Were they real or ghosts?

When I got close to Asa I asked, "Did you see that woman in white?"

Asa boringly replied, "I saw no one but you."

Strange.

Strange indeed.

Or maybe there was nothing strange about it, and Asa couldn't see the people in the shed from where she was standing.

I asked her what she was doing there, how did she know I would be there, and she said, "I saw your picture on the news with your mother. I didn't know that once upon a time she had been a famous author. I Googled her, read about your brother, about his funeral, so I assumed you would be here."

We left the area and made our way to the bus stop. But then we walked past the bus stop and kept on walking along that seemingly endless road, and the rain started to fall down softly, and Asa lit a cigarette, and I lit one too.

A woman dressed in black approached us and asked us where such and such street was, and the two of us shrugged our shoulders. The woman looked tired, and looking at her made me feel tired too.

Asa pulled me by the sleeve and said, "Let's go."

So we kept on walking, with her leading the way. Cars, buses, motorbikes zoomed past us, planes flew above us, people laughed around us, but we kept quiet and we walked and smoked.

After a long time had passed Asa said, "You look tired."

"I am tired," I said.

"Tired of everything."

"I am tired of everything."

"You look sad, too."

"I am sad."

"Depressed, too?"

"Yes."

A police car drove past us and I saw one cop staring at us while the other one kept an eye on the traffic ahead.

Now I'm sitting in Asa's bed while she washes herself. Her rented room is tiny and she only has space for one chair in it, but that chair is filled with books. At the moment she's reading *Wittgenstein's Mistress* by David Markson. She reads most of those authors that my brother used to read plus a few others, too. She reads Murakami, Bolaño, Jáchym Topol, Peixoto, Atwood, Auster, and she only listens to *Drum & Bass* or whatever is called.

A few hours ago we kissed and when I tried to take her trousers off she said, "No."

I apologised and she said, "It's not your fault, but if you want I'll do blowjob."

Her face was dead serious when she said *blowjob*.

"No, that's okay, you don't have to," I said.

"But I want to and I'm good at it."

And then she cried and told me tales of rape, monstrous tales of a child being raped by her own father from the age of 5 until four years ago. Asa was the child. Sometimes we become objects moulded by the actions of others.

I cried too as I listened to her. I cried for her, for Lester, and afterwards she sucked me and I felt her tears on my cock, and then we kissed and her tongue tasted a bit bitter. Salty and bitter, like life.

We sat on the bed and I held her small, thin, fragile body against mine, and then I asked, "When are we going to meet the BogMan?"

She squeezed my hands and said, "Tomorrow."

And now she's having a shower.

After showering, Asa got her sleeping bag ready and said, "Let's go."

And we left.

We ate hamburgers and fries at a restaurant nearby, drank a couple of beers each, and now we're making our way towards an old building. The stars are out and the sky looks lovely, and even though it has been a sad week I feel good and I want to help and love Asa. I know that she has been through a lot, and it might take years for her to leave everything behind her, but I want to be there with her every step of the way. Maybe this is how it feels to be in love; you put that person above everything else.

I hold her hand and I say, "I'm so happy."

"Me too," she says the words mechanically, sounding like a machine that has been programmed to speak.

But she needs time; I know that; she needs time and love for the wounds to heal. And I've got time for her and love to give her.

We jump over a fence. There are signs saying DO NOT ENTER, DANGER, etc., but we ignore the signs.

Inside, the building smells of piss and sweat.

Years ago every single room in this building was filled with office workers, computers on at all times, coffee machines working non-stop throughout the day, and before the computers arrived the workers in here used to write on typewriters, but the typewriters are long gone, same as the workers, and all the other machinery was moved into a bigger - but not necessarily better - building, and now this one is just waiting to be demolished.

We make our way slowly in the dark, up the dirty steps we go, and then we make our way along a corridor filled with dirt, dirt that was left behind by its last occupants, probably crack addicts and other kind of junkies.

We go right up to the top floor, the 7th floor, right to the end of the corridor, and we enter the last room. Someone is already here. I see shapes in the dark, two heads moving around.

Junkies?

The BogMan (and who else)?

A match kisses a candle and then there is light, a bit of light, enough for me to see the faces of the strangers. A Japanese man. A white man. Which of them is the BogMan?

Asa introduces me to them.

"Karl, this is Kazuo and this is Hayden. Hayden and Kazuo, this is Karl with a K," she says, her little private joke wearing thin by now.

Kazuo takes a little bow and Hayden says, "Hey."

"Hey back at you," I say.

I look at them and they look so miserable, pretty depressed. Bloody hell, looking like that I would kill myself too.

What are they doing here at this time?

Kazuo goes back to sleep and Hayden lights a cigarette while Asa puts her things down and gets the sleeping bag ready. Afterwards, we walk up to a window and we smoke side by side while staring at the city.

"What are these men doing here?" I ask.

"They are waiting for the BogMan," she says.

And then we keep on smoking, silently, each of us lost in our own thoughts, and I look at the buildings far away, the dimmed lights of the city still shining bright, and I find myself missing my apartment. But I stay here because I want to meet this BogMan, this destroyer of lives. I flick the ash into the air and I face Asa. Under the light of the moon, her face looks so pretty, and I want to hold her close to me, tenderly so as not to break her fragile body, and I don't want to let go of her.

We crush the cigarettes under our feet and then we go to sleep. There's no snuggling tonight as Asa falls asleep straight away. I hear the snoring around me, the light snoring of the depressed ones. I wonder how the BogMan will look like and what he will tell us and what will these people ask him. I will record it all without anyone knowing, not even Asa, and then I will share the BogMan's identity with the world. At first some people will hate me, but with time the depressed ones will seek help and afterwards they will thank me for it.

In the morning, when I open my eyes, everyone is already awake. For breakfast we have crackers, cigarettes and a bottle of flat Coke. Asa and Kazuo are standing by the window exchanging a few words in Japanese. Hayden is sitting on the floor reading *A Minor Apocalypse* by Tadeusz Konwicki. I remember reading *Moonrise, Moonset* by the same author last year. It was quite a good book.

Once we're done here I'll go home, have an immersion bath, pancakes with syrup, fresh coffee, and afterwards I will sit on the sofa and read something.

"What time will the BogMan be here?" I ask.

Hayden shrugs his shoulders, and then says, "Soon."

Asa and Kazuo stop talking and start towards the centre of the room. Hayden puts the book down and joins them. They hold hands and Asa tells me to join them too.

They look so calm then, as if they are waiting for the end to arrive, the cure for their depression to materialise out of thin air, as if…

Oh my God!

I realise it too late.

I run to the window and I see the men far away getting ready to demolish the building, ready to blow it up, including us.

I look one last time at Asa, Kazuo and Hayden, who remain expressionless as they stare at me while holding hands.

I open the window and shout, "WAIT!"

But it's too late.

The BogMan waits for no one.

The BogMan is Death.

REMEMBERING BRANDON LEE

Three cups of coffee down my throat so early in the morning, combined with two pieces of toast, an early listening of Franny Choi's poetry online, and I'm ready to face the world. (But is the world ready for me? For peace and quiet?)

Outside, the rain falls softly on the ground, and my girlfriend wants to take an umbrella with her even though I know she won't use it, and I tell her so: "You won't use it," but she insists and almost cries, so I give her one and then we make our way to the park.

Up the road we go; the street is deserted,
Turn right; still deserted,
Turn left – deserted,
And another right,
And we see the world in action:
Drivers heading off to work,
The traffic – such madness,
Buses carrying more workers,
Trucks delivering groceries and beer – for tonight and tomorrow.
Children walking to school with their parents.
Crows patrol the park,
The grass is wet, parts of it covered with litter.
For some reason the crows remind me of Brandon Lee,
Son of Bruce, both sadly gone,
And Brandon's death reminds me of a woman that loved me
But whom I didn't love back,
Because love chooses whom we love,
And I didn't love her even though she loved me
So what could I do but leave her unloved?

I spent one night at her place – don't worry: nothing happened between us.

And on the next morning,
On the way to the train station,
I bought the newspaper and found out that Brandon was gone,
Killed accidently on the set of his movie *The Crow*.
(Now I know why the crows reminded me of him).

SEARCHING FOR KENZABURO OE

One morning I woke up with an urge to read something by Kenzaburō Ōe as it had been years since I last had read something by him, a marvellous –and terribly sad- book called *The Silent Cry*, so I went online, wrote Amazon on Google, then wrote Kenzaburō Ōe on Amazon and checked what books I could get. There weren't a lot of books by him in English even though he has been writing for a long time and I ordered his latest one, a book called *The Changeling*, published years ago in Japan but only recently translated into English. Mr Ōe might be a Nobel Prize winner but, unfortunately, he doesn't enjoy the same success as his compatriot Haruki Murakami. Or Yukio Mishima.

Once I ordered the book I went into the kitchen, made a cup of coffee, put two slices of bread in the toaster, and I texted my friend Jaspal, asking if he wanted to meet later on for coffee. Twenty minutes later, while I was in the shower, I got a reply from Jaspal saying, "Sure."

I had to text him again to arrange a place and time to meet and Jaspal's reply was, "Cool."

You would expect more from a writer, wouldn't you? From both of us, right?

While I was in the shower Yoko joined me, grabbed my sleeping penis, and said, "Hmm, you fell asleep last night but this morning you're mine."

I leave the rest to your imagination… but it was good.

I met Yoko at a party thrown by my friend Kyle Summers, a party for a poet called Andrew Sparks, some depressed dude who wrote three books of poetry before giving up writing and then becoming a farmer for a short while. Around that time I was going out with a beautician called Jane Wild, some crazy woman who did a lot of drugs and was into Bondage and Submission; Wild by name, wild by nature; and my latest book *Up Yours!* was riding high in the charts, the movie rights to it had been bought, the names of John Cusack and Mickey Rourke had been mentioned to play the main characters in the book, and I felt untouchable. Or maybe just a bit proud. Or maybe untouchable and proud. Or something that had nothing to do with being untouchable or with pride.

The party was at Kyle's place, a little apartment somewhere downtown that could hardly fit twenty people in its living room but back then it was bursting with people coming from all directions. There was smoke everywhere; back then no one gave a damn about their lungs; plenty of noise and lots of alcohol going around, and the first thing that Jane said to me when we got there was, "I'm just going to the bathroom to powder my nose."

That was a nice way of her saying that she was going to the bathroom to do a line or two of coke. Honestly, I could never understand people's fascination with drugs.

So, just like that, I was left on my own by the front entrance, staring at strangers, a few writers that I knew vaguely from somewhere, a corrupt politician (is there any other kind?), a male agent that once made a pass at me at another party, a porn star; tall, blonde, sexy, big breasts; they too all look the same, just like the politicians (but while the porn star gets screwed, the politician screws us all), and I was wondering what to do, thinking what the hell was I doing there, what the hell was Jane up to, and I was also thinking that it would be a good idea to break up with her soon when Kyle came over to say hello, a big smile on his face, and walking behind him was a tall, slender, Japanese woman. Kyle looked a mess, and anyone could tell it was due to lack of sleep. His khaki pants were in need of being ironed, same as his shirt, but his curly blond hair was looking good as usual, which wasn't a surprise seeing that he spends so much time looking after his hair.

"Hey, you made it!" he said and opened his arms wide before pressing my body against his, hugging me as if we were the best of friends when in fact he wasn't a good friend of mine or even my agent.

From what I've heard, this also at a party, Kyle tried to become a writer once but everything he wrote was deemed unpublishable so he became an agent instead because he wanted to look after true artists. I never read a thing that he wrote (but I was told by those who did that his stuff was really bad) so I can't judge him as a writer, but I can say he's a good agent because both Jaspal Patel and Simon Howels, another good friend of mine, are his clients, and at the time so was Andrew Sparks.

A huge grin on his face, Kyle turned to the Japanese woman and said, "Yoko, this is John Sparks. John, this is Yoko Tanaka."

"Hey, John and Yoko," I said and I looked her in the eye because I wanted her to see that I was the kind of guy who looks women in the eye, a confident guy who's not afraid to show intimacy.

She punched me on the shoulder and said, "Get the fuck out of here!" and then she laughed and said. "Sorry. I always wanted to say that."

We stood there by the door, just the three of us, oblivious to the commotion around us.

Yoko said, "I love your books. *Up Yours!*, *Orgasmic Organic*, *Revenge of the Nerd*; read them all, laughed loads. You're like Garry Shandling. So..." She took a long pause. Was she going to use the S word and say that I was so sarcastic? Sexy maybe? No. Instead she said, "...witty. Yes, that's the word. So witty and funny."

"Prettier than Garry, I hope," I said.

"Oh dear, Garry is gorgeous. I'd rather go out with him and his brain than with some muscular brainless idiot."

"Yeah, me too," I said, trying to use a bit of humour and gain some points.

She laughed again and again, short bursts of laughter, loud laughter, while holding on to my right arm. Sensing that something was about to happen between us, Kyle sensibly walked away, leaving the field open for me, but there was still the small matter of Jane to deal with.

Yoko and I stood by the door, neither of us making an effort to move and join the others, and she told me a bit about herself: Tokyo-born, single, living in Brooklyn for the last 5 years, artist, sometimes wrote haiku, and I kept looking over her shoulder while she told me more about herself. I kept searching for Jane but there was no sign of her, and then I saw another woman go into the bathroom only for that same woman to come running out of it a couple of seconds later and scream, "Someone is overdosing!"

Talking Heads was blasting out of unseen speakers, dozens of mouths were talking at the same time, but, nevertheless, we all heard what she said. But just to make sure we heard it right, she screamed, "SOME BITCH HAS OD!"

I assessed the situation calmly while everyone else seemed to panic; over-dosed Jane or sexy Yoko? Choice quickly made (hey, I was going to break up with Jane anyway), I turned to Yoko and said, "Let's get the hell out of here before the cops arrive."

"But I don't even know you."

"Hey, I'm John, you're Yoko," I said, flashed her my best smile, but, nonetheless, she didn't look that impressed and even stared at me funnily.

"And didn't you come to this party with someone else?" she asked, turning around to look at the commotion.

I was trying my best to get out of there and bring Yoko along with me, and I said, "I met that woman outside..."

Yoko interrupted me and said, "Yeah, let's get the hell out of here."

And that's how I met the beautiful Yoko.

After showering, I put on some clean clothes, and while Yoko went back to her studio to do some work, I went out for a walk. I had ordered a book by Kenzaburō Ōe but I still wanted to read something by him on that same day and not wait 2-3 days for *The Changeling* to arrive, so I set out towards Fulton Street on foot, not bothering to catch a cab.

It was Yoko who introduced me to the writing of Kenzaburō Ōe. A couple of weeks after our first date, our first date being the same day that Jane overdosed (more about her later on), I went to her place in Flatbush, a one-bedroom flat that also served as her studio, and in her small bookshelf I saw a couple of books by Ōe-san; *A Quiet Life* and *Hiroshima Notes*. In the next couple of days, I read them both, one after the other, and after I finished reading them I read some of my favourite authors; Nabokov, Bellow, the Frenchman Joris-Karl Huysmans, and then went back to Kenzaburō Ōe. I found an old copy of *The Silent Cry* at a bookshop on 3rd Avenue, right next to a not-so-old copy of a book of mine called *Cynical Girl*, a book that I wrote under the alias of Debbie Rhodes (yes, I'm Debbie). I bought the book, carried it with me to a café in Borough Park, and then I must have read the next sixty pages without taking my eyes off it. I probably would have stayed there all day reading the book hadn't my phone rang. It was Yoko, wanting to meet, so I left the café and took a cab back to her place.

On Fulton Street I went to a bookshop where a tall, cute girl came to see me straight away and I asked if she had anything by Kenzaburō Ōe.

"Who?" she asked and I repeated the name, Kenzaburō Ōe, quite slowly, and the cute girl looked at me weirdly, probably wondering if I was making fun of her.

"Never heard of him," she said.

"He's a Japanese author."

"We've got a couple of books by Haruki Murakami and Banana Yoshimoto."

"Yes but I want Kenzaburō Ōe."

"Are you sure?"

"Of course I'm sure."

"You look familiar. Are you famous?"

"A bit. I'm a writer."

"You're not that Ōe guy, are you?"

"Do I look Japanese?"

"Is that a trick question?"

"No."

"In that case, no."

I walked out of there without having any luck.

I made my way to Vanderbilt Avenue, walked past Joyce Bakeshop, the place where I met Jane, and went to another bookshop where, again, I asked if they had anything by Kenzaburō Ōe. The man that saw to me was in his mid-forties and he looked like the kind of person who would know his literature so I was feeling quite optimistic. But the guy asked, "Who?"

"Kenzaburō Ōe," I said.

"Ōe. Ōe. Never heard of him."

"He won the Nobel Prize in Literature in 1994," I said.

"Fuck me, this is 2013. Who cares about 1994?"

Another guy, younger than the one who was talking to me, let out a short laugh.

"He's a very famous Japanese writer," I said.

The young guy turned around and said, "Hey, I like Murakami."

"Haruki?" I asked.

"No. Ryu. Ryu Murakami," the young guy replied.

"Yeah, I like Murakami too," the older guy said.

"Ryu?" I asked.

23

"Nah. Haruki," said the older guy.

I felt like I was having a dialogue with the Marx Brothers or Laurel and Hardy.

And then the older guy told me they had books by Natsuo Kirino, Shuichi Yoshida, Banana Yoshimoto, Ryu Murakami, Haruki Murakami, Natsume Soseki, Yoko Ogawa, etc., but no Kenzaburō Ōe.

I thanked them for their time and left the shop feeling tired, and then I made my way to another bookshop, this time on 7ᵗʰ Avenue, and when I entered the shop I was greeted by a cute teenager, probably not even twenty-years-old, and I knew I probably would have no luck in finding a book by Kenzaburō Ōe. Nevertheless, I asked slowly, as if I was talking to a child: "I'm looking for a book by a Japanese writer, and, please, don't say Murakami."

"Ryu or Haruki?" the young woman said and smiled.

Good. A joker. I like that. (Not really.)

"Actually, as far as I know, he's the only Japanese writer to have won the Nobel Prize in Literature," I said.

"You're wrong there because two Japanese writers have won the Nobel Prize in Literature; Yasunari Kawabata and Kenzaburō Ōe," the young woman said, sounding a bit proud of herself.

Of course. Kawabata. *Snow Country*, *Beauty and Sadness*, *The Master of Go*. How could I have forgotten him?

"So, you know who Kenzaburō Ōe is?" I asked, and she looked at me as if I was dumb, and then she rolled her eyes. She then excused herself because she had to see to two customers, but told me to wait and I said okay.

I scanned the bookshelves, the letters O and K, the foreign books, even the romance sections and biographies, but no Kenzaburō Ōe anywhere. Plenty of Haruki Murakami though, both on the fiction section and even on the shelves dedicated to biographies as he had some kind of memoir out about marathons or running or something of that sort. While I was browsing through the shelves, the young woman disappeared into a backroom and returned shortly afterwards with two books, both by Kenzaburō Ōe.

"New stock," she said.

The books were *The Silent Cry*, which I already had, and *The Changeling*, which I had ordered from Amazon. I told her I already had *The Silent Cry* and I was also going to say no to *The Changeling* since I had ordered it in the morning, but then I browsed through a couple of pages and I knew I had to buy it.

Mission accomplished, I set off to Starbucks on 7th Avenue where I was going to meet Jaspal. My legs were aching but I was feeling a bit inspired, and after ordering an iced coffee I sat down, pulled out a notebook from my right coat pocket, and I started to write some notes down for a new book. I would call it *Coming From Behind* and it would be some sort of memoir, as is almost every book and story that I wrote although I always change the names and the places so that no one knows whom I'm writing about.

Jaspal arrived thirty minutes later than the arranged time and then he complained about train delays, as he always does, and about cab drivers who couldn't speak English, and I told him about my day and about my search for a Kenzaburō Ōe book, and he said, "Ōe? I'm reading him right now."

Then, as if by magic, he produced a book by Kenzaburō Ōe out of his bag, a book called *Somersault*.

"Strange book," he said. "So unlike his other work."

Someone I know from some place entered *Starbucks* alongside a pretty blonde and he waved at me and I waved back, and then I looked at Jaspal and said, "I know that guy from somewhere."

"Which guy?" Jaspal scanned the café.

"The one by the counter with the pretty blonde," I said.

"That's Andrew Sparks, the poet turned novelist-teacher. I don't know who the blonde is. Maybe she's his new girlfriend. Hey, are you guys related?"

"Not that I know."

"Oh, I just thought, you know, same surname; John Sparks, Andrew Sparks."

"A lot of sparks."

"Yeah, be careful or you might set the place on fire."

"I thought he was a farmer now," I said.

"I guess it's easier to write a book than to take a carrot out of your arse. Anyway, from what I've heard, one day Andrew woke up alone in his little farm out there in the middle of nowhere, away from the noise and the city lights, and then, for some reason, he panicked, and weeks later, after having sold his farm and got his old job back, he was back in the city, teaching literature somewhere downtown or uptown, and he has also written some conspiracy book called *The Net Effect*, or something like that."

"How do you go from writing poetry to writing conspiracy books?" I asked and I looked again at the former poet, former farmer, now turned conspiracy-thriller writer. He looked to be in fine shape, dressed trendily in a grey suit and white shirt, the last two buttons unbuttoned at the top to show off his tan. The pretty blonde sitting next to him was sucking slowly on a straw, the tip of her tongue coming in and out of her mouth, and she kind of reminded me of a young Bardot; a mixture of naivety and beauty, but Andrew looked like a mixture of arrogance and maturity, and I wondered what he was doing with a girl like that.

"Who knows? I guess he has written all the poems he could master out of his head and now he has decided to go where the big bucks are and step into Dan Brown territory," said Jaspal.

"It's like Dante suddenly becoming Dan Brown," I said.

I looked around the café as I searched for more familiar faces but I saw no one that I know. A lot of the people at the café were glued to their personal computers or tablets or iPhones or whatever, and a young woman on her own was reading a book by Marybeth Hicks called *Bringing up Geeks*. That's what my mother did.

We left Starbucks before Andrew and his companion but we never went over to his table to say hello or anything because neither I nor Jaspal were that close to the former poet.

Outside Starbucks Jaspal touched my shoulder and said, "I almost forgot to tell you who I saw the other day. That crazy ex of yours, Jane Wild."

"Jane?" I hadn't seen Jane since that night when she overdosed on cocaine. I know that she was taken to the hospital where she remained for a few days until her parents came to get her, and a few weeks later, once I was already in a proper relationship with Yoko, Jane called and said, "You fuck! You cruel bastard! You dickless piece of shit! You..."

The name calling went on for a long time and instead of hanging up on her I kept on listening to her as she called me every single dirty name that she could think of. Maybe I took it all as some kind of punishment for having walked out on her.

After a good ten minutes she hanged up the phone and that was it. I never heard from her ever since then.

"How is she?" I asked.

"She's good. She has her own beauty clinic where my wife Lucy goes and from what I've heard she also has a book coming out soon called *Wild Life*."

"Shit! A memoir?"

Jaspal shrugged his shoulders and said, "Maybe. You know how it is in this damn city; everyone wants to be a writer or some kind of superstar."

Oh no. What were the chances of her not mentioning me in her book?

We parted ways not that far from *Starbucks* and this time I took a cab back to Yoko's place. When I got home Yoko was out so I sat on the sofa where I dozed off for a couple of hours.

I woke up to the sound of coffee being ground. Yoko was back and she was in the kitchen preparing something for us to eat. I took my time getting up from the sofa. With every movement that I made I heard a bone snap. It had been months since I last exercised, unless you count the endless walks that I take around New York (and the sex marathons with Yoko), and living the life of a writer; sitting down for hours in front of a small screen or scribbling down, wasn't the best way to stay fit. Luckily I was born with fit genes and there wasn't a lot of fat accumulating around my waist. Still, I should do a bit more of exercise.

Yoko smiled when she saw I was up and said, "I've got something for you."

She shuffled around her bag and took out a book.

"I heard you saying you wanted to get a new book by Kenzaburō Ōe so I got you this one," she said, handing me a copy of *The Changeling*.

I didn't have the heart to tell her I already had a copy of the same book with me and another one in order.

Oh well, at least now I know what to give to a couple of friends as birthday presents.

THE LIFE OF
A NOVELIST
(For Henry Roth)

The clock hasn't yet reached 5 a.m. but he has already been up for more than one hour sitting in front of his desk, typing slowly on his computer. He's tired but he'll try to write for another hour before he jumps in the shower and gets ready for work. Last year Elias Piëch published his second novel, a romance called *Reflections on the way to Death*, and it had good reviews, just like his first novel, *Broken Mirrors*, but it was still a flop, just like his first book, both released by an independent publisher, and, as of yet, Elias can't make a living as a writer and he has to work in that stupid kitchen which he hates so much.

Last week he got into a fight with one of the chefs because the other man provoked him. First, the chef said, "Hey Elias, why don't you write a book about washing dishes?"

Elias didn't reply but for some reason —maybe jealousy- the chef really wanted to provoke Elias, and afterwards he said, "What a loser. I'm surprised your woman is still with you."

Elias kept quiet but then the chef said, "I bet she fucks around with other guys," and that's when Elias lost his head and punched the chef on the face. Luckily for him no one saw what happened, and the chef was too proud and embarrassed to say anything about the incident to anyone, or so Elias thought, and after the punch, the other man simply got up and went back to work. And so did Elias but he didn't forget what happened because the novelist records everything in his head, or at least the events which he thinks will matter.

By the time he leaves home his girlfriend Claire is already up, smoking a Gauloise in the kitchen, and she looks disinterested when he kisses her goodbye. The novelist is no fool and he can tell she's not happy with her life, with him, with the way things are turning out to be. When they met great things were expected of him. By then he already had published a couple of stories in a few magazines, had been mentioned on Granta, The Guardian, and a few blogs too, but two years gone past, and two books published, Elias Piëch still remains a nobody in the world of literature, a world that is populated with millions of other writers who walk in vain – for years, if not decades - in the darkness that is ignorance; ignorance of their work, that is. His work has been praised, true, but praise doesn't pay the bills, and it certainly doesn't buy Claire the clothes she wants, and, little by little, she's becoming tired of life as a novelist's girlfriend. Last year Elias made close to $2000 from his writing but the year before his earnings (as a novelist) didn't even reach $300. He made a bit more on the side by writing a few articles and book reviews, but, as Claire so nicely put it, "The money you earn as a novelist isn't even enough to buy a decent coffee machine."

He sighed and kept on writing, hoping that soon his work(s) would be widely read, but, as of yet, he's still writing, and not a lot of people seem to be that interested in his work.

He walks to work. He has an old Volvo which he only uses on the odd occasion, like when he goes to the supermarket or on a trip, but he usually walks to work. It's only a twenty minute walk from his home to his workplace and he needs the exercise. Claire also doesn't drive to work. Usually she gets the bus and at night a colleague drops her home. She works as a receptionist at a dental practice. The job is boring but she still earns more than Elias. Lately she has been thinking about leaving him. She has applied for a few jobs in the City to work as a legal secretary, the subject she studied, and the money is good, a lot more than what she's earning now, and the City has always been her dream destination so she's waiting for a reply with crossed fingers. A friend of hers has her own place in the City and she told Claire she's welcome to stay with her for as long as she wants and needs, and all Claire needs now is a positive reply from one of the places she applied for.

She finishes her coffee and goes to the bathroom. She turns on the hot water and gets in the bath while the water runs slowly down her body. She touches herself, softly at first, softly and slowly, but then she gathers rhythm and keeps going at it until she comes. Satisfied, if only briefly and temporarily, she dries herself and then gets changed, ready for work, and on the way out she gets a call from someone who wants to interview her for one of the positions she applied for in the City. She smiles. So far, so good.

Mike, the chef that got punched by Elias, is talking with Adrian and Tracey, the owners of the restaurant, when the novelist walks in.

The novelist says nothing apart from good morning, and neither do they (apart from good morning), but he knows that they are – or were - talking about him. He also fears that after today, or probably by the end of the month, he'll have no job either. A few hours later he's told by Tracey that they will have to let him go as they don't have any more use for his services. As a parting shot she says, "Maybe is better this way. Maybe you can finally write a bestseller."

She sneers and grins but is disappointed when Elias simply walks away without making a fuss. He takes one last look at Mike who avoids his eyes, and then he leaves the restaurant. Nicole, one of the waitresses, is the only one who comes running after him to say goodbye. She hugs him outside the restaurant and says, "Take care, Elias. If you ever need anything, just a friend to chat with, give me a call."

He looks at her, at the piece of paper she's holding in her hands which she then hands over to him, at the faces behind her, faces that are staring at them; Mike, Tracey, Adrian, and so many others, and he feels relieved for knowing that he is leaving them all behind. He thanks Nicole, and once she goes inside the restaurant he turns his back on her, on all of them, and walks away.

On the way home he stops by a bookstore and buys an old copy of *Man's Fate*, by André Malraux. He crosses the road and goes to the bank to check his account and savings. It's not much but he has enough to last him for a few months. At least Claire has her job and Elias will also get some benefits now that he has lost his job. If anything, this will also be the push he needs to look for a better job. But the dream... the dream of becoming a successful and famous novelist is slowly slipping away.

"But think of Henry Roth," he thinks. "Look how long it took him."

That night, to Elias' surprise, Claire takes the news quite well but he doesn't know that she's thinking about leaving him. A few days later, she tells him she has to go to the City to visit her friend Martha and he says okay. In the morning, once she's gone, he goes to the job centre, applies for a few jobs, and then he goes home and reads for a bit. Afterwards he sits at his desk and goes through the notes for his new book. He reads it slowly but he doesn't like what he's reading. It's written in a beautiful tone of voice but it's not him. He puts the notes aside and takes another notepad from one of the drawers in his desk.

Outside, it is raining heavily and he wonders how – and what - Claire is doing in the City. The water in the kettle is boiled and he goes into the kitchen to make a cup of coffee. While in there he also eats two slices of bread with butter. He stays in the kitchen for another hour, drinking coffee and reading Malraux.

Around 6 p.m., feeling bored and with nothing to do, he goes out for a walk around town. A couple of people greet him because they have seen him in a magazine and know that he has written a couple of books, but neither of them has read any of his work, not even the interview he gave to the magazine.

He bumps into Nicole outside *Starbucks* and she invites him for a drink. At *Starbucks* she drinks a latte and he drinks a hot chocolate. The place is filled with students glued to their laptops and he sees a couple of people reading, but neither of them is reading his books. One of them is reading *Crow*, a book of poems by Ted Hughes, and the other person is reading *Stoner* by John Williams. Even Nicole has a book with her; something by Theodore Roethke, and when she sees him staring at the book she asks, "How is your writing going?"

"Bad," he replies coldly, sounding indifferent to her question.

Unknown to Elias, Nicole has had feelings for him for quite a long time but because she knows that he's in a relationship with Claire she has kept those feelings hidden.

When they finally leave the café he feels a lot better, in part thanks to Nicole's company, and he walks her home. Outside her building she invites him in but warns him that her place is a bit of a mess, but he declines her invitation, saying, "Maybe some other time," and after thanking her for a quiet, relaxed afternoon, he walks home. On the way home he can't stop thinking about Nicole.

That night he neither reads nor writes and goes to bed quite early, falls asleep straight away, and he's up before 4 a.m. After the morning piss, he grabs a notepad and a pen, and carries it with him into the kitchen where he writes for three straight hours. At 9 a.m. he leaves home and goes to the local library, not to get any books but for a job interview. The interview goes well and he feels happy with himself when he leaves the library. He goes straight home and when he gets there Claire is in the living room waiting for him. By the look on her face he can tell she has something to say and it's not something good. She puts on a sympathetic smile, bordering on pity, and she asks, "How was your day?"

"Good. I just returned from a job interview. It's to work in the library. They'll let me know in a few days if the job is mine. The money isn't great but it pays more than washing dishes," he says. Then he asks, "How was it in the City?"

"It was good. It was really good," she says and her face seems to radiate with joy when he mentions the City. "Actually, we need to talk about it."

When she says that, he gets ready for the worst. Their relationship has been a bit unstable for quite a while and Elias knows that Claire isn't really happy to be living with him. As early as two years ago, she wanted to move out of their town, and she even told him that a move to the City would be good for his writing, but Elias kept delaying it because he really doesn't like the City. The three times he went there; twice to give interviews and once for a book signing event along with other authors, he found the place dull, filled with cold people, snobbish creatures that lived cold lives, and the only thing people did there was smoke, drink, go to parties, have lots of sex with different people, do drugs, try hard to become rich and famous, and everyone was trying (too) hard to become famous, be a star, even if many of them lacked any real talent. Now Claire's telling him what he feared for a while; she's moving on without him, moving to the City to start a new life, moving by the end of the month, but she's moving out of his place tonight because she can't bear to be in there for a minute longer. So much for true love.

Elias doesn't know what to say. What can he say?

After she says all she has to say, she leaves him on his own on the sofa and goes to pack her bags. The moment she heard she got the job she made a few calls to get things moving forward. She called her parents first to tell them the good news and to ask them if she could stay with them for a couple of weeks before moving to the City, and afterwards she called her friend in the City to tell her the good news too, and, more importantly, to ask her if she could stay with her, and her friend said, "Yeah, sure. You're going to love life in the City."

She puts all her clothes in a bag and when she returns to the living room to get her books and CDs Elias is nowhere to be seen. At first she thinks he's in the kitchen or in the bathroom, but after looking for him for a few seconds she realises he's gone out.

"Maybe it's better this way," she thinks. She finishes packing quickly and then calls for her father to pick her up.

Her parents are glad to see her back at their place even if it's only for a short while, and they're even happier to know that she left *that boring Jewish writer* behind once and for all.

The novelist leaves the building but he doesn't go that far. He crosses the road and goes inside a café that is owned by a friend of his. The novelist is hungry so he orders chicken soup with Kreplach, followed by knish, and he drinks a glass of carrot juice, followed by an espresso. While he's in the café he sees Claire's father arrive and then watches as they both carry everything into a van. And then she's off, out of his life, and when the van is finally out of sight he feels a lump in his throat, and he finds it hard to breathe for a few seconds, but he quickly puts the pain away, the pain and the anger, and when he steps out of the café he goes to the park for a walk instead of heading straight home. He can't bear to go home, not yet anyway, and find the place empty; every piece of Claire gone, everything but the memory of her.

The park is almost empty but he sees the familiar face of Nicole standing by the river on her own, feeding the ducks, and he approaches her slowly. A couple sitting on a bench greet him. They are among the few readers of his works, the woman having read both his books. Elias greets them back and when Nicole hears his voice she turns around and watches him as he exchanges small talk with the couple.

The sky is clear now, the sun is out, unlike a couple of hours ago when a few dark clouds patrolled the sky and the weather looked as if it was going to take a turn for the worse.

A young boy of four and a young girl of five run in circles around a tree while their mother sits on the grass, and Elias stares at them for a few seconds, wondering if he will ever be a father. Afterwards he joins Nicole who is so happy to see him but the novelist is feeling too sad to notice the happiness on Nicole's face. He watches her as she feeds the ducks, they talk for a bit, ten minutes or so, and afterwards he walks her home. On the way back to her place she tells him a bit more about herself and he finds out that she's doing some sort of degree on Child Psychology. She also asks him how he's doing, is he working on a new book, how is the job search going, and he tells her about his job interview at the library and how he's having a bit of a writer's block, but he never mentions Claire leaving him.

This time Nicole doesn't invite him in and they shake hands outside her home, but when she's about to enter the building he says, "If I get the job, let's celebrate."

She smiles and says okay, and then, to her surprise, he kisses her right cheek. She blushes, if only for a bit (but enough for Elias to notice it), and the novelist says, "See you later."

"See you later," she whispers, dreamlike, and she watches him walk away.

Ten minutes later, when the novelist gets home and notices the pieces of Claire missing everywhere he looks; on the shelves and around him, on the sofa, her mug gone, and he feels a bit sick, overcome with nausea, but the feeling is only temporary because on that same afternoon he gets a call from the library saying that they would love for him to start work next week. He jumps in the air and screams a silent yes. On that same night he calls Nicole to tell her the good news, mentioning also that Claire left him, and then he starts work on his third novel which he calls *Last on Line*, a novel which will be some sort of biography about himself and his parents and other members of his family.

The first month in the City goes well for Claire and once she gets her first pay check she moves into a studio of her own. Living with her friend was wearing her out and she could hardly wait to move out. But on the second month, once the novelty of living in the City wears out, she finds herself missing Elias, their small town, and their friends, too. At her workplace everyone has their own agenda and she finds it hard to socialise with her colleagues and to get to know them well. With time she starts living a boring life, and after being in the City for only six months she starts thinking about moving out, but her career is going well and six months into her job she gets a pay increase so she stays on for another month, and another, and time moves on ever so slowly.

Sometimes she searches for Elias online just to see what he's up to, what new works has he released, but the novelist seems to have run out of ideas and no one even mentions him online, and Claire is too embarrassed to ask her parents or friends back home about him.

One Friday night, while having dinner on her own, she almost chokes on a piece of meat, and for the next few seconds, as she tries to swallow it or cough it out, she thinks that she's going to die alone.

Luckily she manages to cough the food out but she's scared to eat anything else and just lies on the floor crying. That same night she calls her parents to tell them what happened, and then, while still on the phone, she bursts into tears and screams, "I'm going to die alone! I'm going to die alone!"

Her mother is panicking while the father is telling both women to calm down. After a few minutes of crying Claire manages to calm down but on the next day she asks her father to come and get her.

Two years have gone past since he released his second novel and the name of Elias Piëch is slowly being forgotten by the world of literature, which doesn't come as a surprise since he was never that famous, but in that same year he finally releases the first of a four-part volume *Last on Line*, the first volume being called *The Ghost of Prague*, a chronicle of his life in Prague, the death of his parents, and his departure from his country alongside his uncles. To his surprise and delight, the book is met with success, both critically and commercially. The second volume of *Last on Line*, called *Empathy*, chronicling his life in a new country, comes out nine months after the first volume and again it is a success, outselling even the first volume.

Once Claire was gone the novelist found himself writing even more because he wanted to be too busy to even think about her. On that same week he also went out with Nicole, only dinner (and nothing else happened), and a few days later he started to work at the library. The job was good, not too hard either but he didn't mind hard work, and he enjoyed being there. Sometimes he would have to put up with some sneers or idiotic remarks due to his failure as a novelist, but he kept cool about it and just got on with his job. He started to meet Nicole on a more regular basis, and after a month or so of going out as friends they started dating, and three months later she moved in with the novelist. His apartment, inherited from his uncles, was quite spacious, the large living room filled with ceiling-high shelves, books everywhere, but although it was spacious and clean, the place lacked a feminine touch which Nicole, unlike Claire, brought with her. She bought enormous plant pots which gave the place a cosier look, enlarged pictures of Elias and his family and them both, framed them, and then covered some of the blank walls with picture frames, and with time the apartment became a cosy home for a couple in love. To the dismay of her parents, who were both atheists, Nicole joined Elias' faith, which meant she converted to Judaism. After going out with Nicole for a year Elias asked for her hand in marriage. Somehow it felt like the right thing. They got married and Nicole's parents gave her their blessing, and they lived happily ever after. Or did they?

The novelist kept on working on his big book and he also found a new job as an accountant for a small firm, a job that paid him more than what he was earning at the library, and the working hours were less which meant he had more time for his writing and also for Nicole.

As faith would have it, his new job was just opposite the restaurant where he used to work washing dishes and from where he was unfairly sacked, and some days he would bump into Mike, the chef he punched and who got him fired, but Elias didn't hold any grudge towards the other man, and instead of ignoring him he greeted him, and Mike, feeling a bit ashamed of his past behaviour towards the novelist, greeted him back.

Claire wakes up late, a few minutes after 10 a.m., and she feels refreshed. Two days back in town, stuck inside her parents' house, back in her old bedroom, and she feels good, better than she has in a long time. Her parents are at work, finishing their shifts at 5 p.m. and 6 p.m., which means she has the whole house for herself. This morning, once she showers and gets changed, she goes out, and the first person she goes to see is the novelist. She walks towards his building, past the post office where old Joe, the postman, greets her, past the butchers and bakery where again a few people greet her, and she feels glad to be back, to know that she belongs somewhere, and you always know you belong somewhere when everyone greets you. It is Saturday and she hopes to find the novelist at home. As she gets closer to his place Claire feels her body getting a bit warm, her cheeks and ears turn red, her knees wobble a bit, and she wonders how Elias will react when he sees her, but she keeps on moving forward, towards the building where he lives. She crosses the road, excitement and fear running through her, and as she gets closer to the front door she wonders what she will say to Elias if he is home, and what will he say when he sees her?

She rings the buzzer and waits, half worried, half excited. She's about to press the buzzer for a second time when Mr. Krauss, Elias's neighbour on the second floor, steps out of the building. He recognises her straight away and wonders what she's doing there because, as far as he remembers, she left the novelist ages ago and he now has someone else. He wonders if she made a love mistake, one of those mistakes that can't be fixed by time. She greets him and asks about Elias, and a reluctant Mr. Krauss tells her the novelist is away on honeymoon.

"Honeymoon?" a shocked Claire says back.

"Yes. He got married last week and went to Prague for his honeymoon," says Mr. Krauss, and then he looks at his watch and says he's in a rush to get to the synagogue.

Off he goes while Claire remains there on her own, still as a statue, her face now a mixture of confusion and horror, but once the shock dies down she walks away in anger, angry at the novelist for having married so quickly the moment she left him. That afternoon she cries for a long time, out of desperation, out of anger, and once the tears dry up she lies in bed for a few minutes, her head spinning with too many thoughts running past her at the speed of light. What she can't understand is why Elias married the other woman so quick but never spoke about marriage while he was going out with her. That really makes her jealous. Furious, too. But even if he had asked her to marry him back then she probably would have said no.

A few days later the novelist is back along with his wife. While on honeymoon he wrote nothing but once he's at home, and once the wife falls asleep, he returns to his big book. He tries to write at least ten pages a day, but some days he writes more than that and some days less. But he does make an effort to write at least ten pages a day. Or more.

Claire finds a job in a furniture shop owned by a friend of her father. The job is easy, much easier and less hectic than the one she had in the City, and the money is also less but she doesn't need that much to survive in her town. But she needs a man, she needs love, and the one (love/man) she had has someone else now and Claire isn't too happy about it.

One Thursday afternoon Elias bumps into Claire outside his workplace, this happening four days after he had gone back to work. He already knew Claire was back in town but he didn't know she had been watching him ever since he returned from honeymoon, and her bumping into him is no coincidence. But she still pretends that it is and she even says, "Elias. What a coincidence. I heard you got married. Congratulations."

The novelist is taken aback when he sees her. He was deeply hurt when she left but Nicole quickly helped him forget Claire, and he came to the conclusion that he really didn't love her, but he's still a bit confused, not to mention quite uncomfortable in the presence of this woman with whom he lived with for such a long time. Claire asks him if he has time for a quick drink just so they can catch up on lost time, but he excuses himself and says he has to go.

"No problem. Maybe some other time," she says, smiling sheepishly at him.

"Yes, maybe some other time," Elias says before rushing out of there.

Claire thinks that the reason why the novelist is in such a rush to leave is because he feels awkward to see her, and she thinks wrongly that he still has feelings for her. And while she watches him walk away she feels a longing for him, for his hands all over her body, and she wants him back at all costs.

She heads home feeling rejected, rejected by love, by life, and she feels as if a big prank has been played on her and as if everybody is laughing at her. At home she locks herself in her room and slaps her face repeatedly while cursing everyone silently. Before she goes to sleep she makes a promise that if she can't have Elias, then no one else will have him either.

The novelist writes more and more every day and Nicole asks him to slow down, relax, sleep a bit more, and the novelist smiles before kissing her. He writes a chapter about his first love, his first fight with an anti-Semite at school, a fight he won but on the next day the anti-Semite came looking for him alongside three friends and Elias had to show them how fast he could run; he writes about that too, and he also writes about his uncles, his parents, love and unity, hate and prejudice, and at times, while he's working on his book of memories, the novelist feels consumed by an enormous sadness.

Nicole looks at the size of the book he's writing, a book that never seems to end, and she says, "I've married Proust."

The novelist puts the pen aside and stares at her. And then he says, "Why Proust? Why not Henry Roth? He wrote a big book too; *Mercy of a Rude Stream*, a book that tends to be overlooked by millions."

"You're right," Nicole says and puts her arms around him. "I actually read *Call It Sleep* not so long ago."

He says nothing and kisses her.

Many nights Claire goes out for a walk and she always finds herself standing outside the building where the novelist lives. Her body and heart drive her there even though she's trying (not too) hard to forget him. She lights cigarette after cigarette and stands there, in the cold, rain falling down on her, whatever the weather is, she stands there, staring at the building, at the apartment where the novelist lives with his wife, and sometimes she sees their figures walking past the window, and she hates them. She hates them because she loves him. She hates them because she lost her love. And when that happens, when the hate grows, she says she will get even, but she keeps delaying her revenge.

Book two out of the way, the novelist starts working on book three, simply called *Time*, and he also sends a manuscript of volume one to his agent who upon reading it calls him back straight away and says, "This is the one! Get the champagne ready."

Being quite familiar with failure and disillusion the novelist tries not to get his hopes too high. But he too believes *this is the one*.

Claire hates him now! She really does! She hates him and she loves him. Every week now, for the past year, she walks past him and greets him, or past him and waves, and although Elias greets her too he's always a bit aloof, always a bit distant. And to make things even worse, his wife is now pregnant.

"They will both pay," Claire thinks to herself. "Everyone will pay for my misery."

She starts following the writer and his wife; one day she follows one and the next day she follows the other.

When the hardback copy of *The Ghost of Prague* comes out Elias prepares for the worst, the worst being failure, but this time he's met with success. A month later he becomes a father for the first time.

By now Claire is going mad and has even got herself a gun. She sees the novelist everywhere; on the cover of a magazine, in town, even in her dreams, and she can't believe that she lost it all; the novelist, his success, the chance of having his kids.

She fantasies about killing him and dancing on top of his dead body, kill him and his wife, him and his wife and their baby, too. Her parents notice how she's changing and they try to talk to her, but she's always acting strange, always moody, and she doesn't want to talk to anyone.

Every single night she goes out, gun in her coat pocket, and her destination is always the same. And then she stands outside the building where the novelist lives, her right hand squeezing the gun inside her coat pocket.

The novelist quits his job a month before *Empathy* comes out. Due to the success of *The Ghost of Prague* he can now dedicate his time to full-time writing. As for Nicole, after she finishes her studies and gives birth, she puts her career on hold and stays at home with the novelist and their child.

Consumed by a burning jealousy and hatred towards the novelist - and his wife and son- Claire starts looking for a place to rent near their home. She looks and looks, and waits and waits, for months, mind you, with the jealousy eating her guts, corrupting her mind and soul, until she finally can't take it no more and goes to Elias' apartment, armed; hate and jealousy showing her the path towards the novelist's place. She loaded the gun at home and now she wants to empty it on the novelist and on his family, and if she has to, she will reload it and empty it on whoever gets in her way.

Since his career as a novelist is going well now, a lot better than he expected, Elias starts thinking about moving into a bigger place, a nice house with a back garden where his son can play and Nicole and he can grow plants and vegetables as they always dreamed. He sits down with Nicole and tells her of his plans to move on to a bigger place, and she says, "Yes. Let's move out of this town. I'm sick of seeing your ex spying on us."

"Who? Claire?" he asks and Nicole nods yes.

He gets up from his chair and asks, "How come you never said a thing about it?"

"I didn't want to worry you," she says.

"Well, now I'm worried," he says and walks to the window. He peers through the curtains and sees Claire standing on the other side of the road. She doesn't look too happy.

Quickly, he closes the curtains, hoping that Claire hasn't seen him, and turns to face Nicole.

"She's there! She's outside!" he says.

"She's always outside," Nicole says.

She crosses the road fast. Mr. Krauss is about to enter the building when Claire brushes past him, almost knocking the old man in the process. He shouts, "Hey!" but she ignores him and keeps on walking, and once the old man gathers himself together he goes after her. Once she's inside the building, she takes the gun out of her pocket and holds it firmly and tightly behind her back. She goes up the steps, those steps she knows so well, and then she walks along the corridor, determined to put an end to the novelist's life.

And his wife.

And their child.

She knocks on the door three times. Then bangs on it furiously.

No reply.

She wonders if Elias is hiding inside and she's about to shoot the door when she hears footsteps behind her. She turns around, gun in her right hand, sees Mr. Krauss who stops in his tracks when he sees the gun and, shaking, he says, "The novelist moved out."

"What?" Claire screams, and a visibly disturbed and scared Mr. Krauss says, "The novelist moved out."

"When?"

"This morning."

"Where to?"

"I think he went to Brooklyn first but I don't know if he's going to stay there permanently."

"What?" she screams and gives her back to the old man who, slowly, makes his way into his apartment and locks the door behind him. He runs to the telephone to call the police while he hears the screaming in the corridor, the screams of a frantic, crazy woman, followed by a single shot.

The novelist is putting the final touches to *Time*, the third volume of *Last on Line*, when he gets the phone call. Nicole is in the kitchen with their child. Elias answers the phone and then he listens to what happened to Claire and realises how lucky he was having left his old place just in time.

For the next few weeks his ex-girlfriend's name is on the news.

The novelist hears and reads about Claire's suicide, and then he hears how she was obsessed with him. Journalists go into the room where she was living and they see pictures of the novelist everywhere, alone or with his family, pictures glued to the walls of the tiny room where Claire lived, in her drawers, inside books he wrote.

The novelist listens to the tales of a jealous and obsessed woman, reads about it, and even gives a few interviews about her, and afterwards, once the madness dies down, he sits down in front of his desk and starts writing the last volume of *Last on Line* simply called *Live(s)*, a book about his life with and without Claire. And he writes about it because that's what a novelist does.

THE TYPEWRITER

Sitting in a café drinking tea.
The poet sitting on the table next to me
Is writing on a typewriter.
A red Olivetti;
A beautiful shining Valentine.
I want to get up and touch its keys.
Take it home with me
And lie naked in bed with my arms wrapped around it.
The sound of its keys reminds me of days gone past.
Days gone past remind me of you.
You remind me of sadness.

When we were together
We used to read Kerouac and Fante,
Later on, Plath and Dante.
Now I read Dufresne and Basho,
Cortázar and Bolaño.
Who knows what you read these days.

We used to share a typewriter,
Fight over it while living in a cold room,
And then, while one typed,
The other one wrote by hand.

Our room smelled of coffee and cigarettes,
Love and despair.
You were the poet,
I was the narrator.
I was in love but you were not.

One day you left and took the typewriter with you.
I kept on writing and I filled notebooks with your name.
Nowadays I no longer write about you
But today I wrote this.
It's not about you.
Really, it's not.
It's about the typewriter we shared.
It was a Smith Corona,

Faded black,
And its keys made a beautiful sound.
What a lovely machine it was.

The poet keeps on typing
And I finish my coffee.
Outside, the snow is melting
And the pavements are slippery.
I hope I won't fall when I go out
And hurt my pride.
What would the poet write about if I fell on the snow?

DOORS THAT LEAD NOWHERE

José was a good friend of mine, a very good friend indeed, someone I knew from a young age, but we weren't lovers or anything like that. I'm straight, as straight as they come.

Okay, I'll admit it: I had the odd homosexual affair, just to experiment, you know, kill the curiosity, but how many so-called straight men haven't done the same?

We - José and I - met at a poetry reading, this happened so many years ago, decades I should say, which shows you how time flies, and what good days they were then, and I can't believe how things turned out to be, and I can't believe he's gone.

He was born in 1910, me in 1930, which made him 20 years older than me, a man of the world even though he hardly ever left Cuba; two trips only made by him, the destinations Jamaica and Mexico, but the poet knew the whole world by heart.

Nowadays Cubans still talk about him, referring to him as one of the greatest poets of Latin American literature, but he was also a novelist, an author. Yes, sir, give credit to José where it's due.

Recently I re-read *Paradiso* and *Oppiano Licario*, his two masterpieces, both books still unknown to most modern readers. I remember not so long ago, probably at my last year at the university, before I lost all my marbles, metaphorically of course because I have no marbles to lose, a student of mine approached me and started to talk about Roberto Bolaño and *The Savage Detectives*, and he said the Chilean was finally opening the doors of Latin American literature, and then I mentioned José to my student and he had the nerve to ask, "Who?"

My face turned red, it became a face filled with anger, and the student took a few steps backwards before retreating silently.

I'm old now. I hardly ever leave this small apartment of mine. A couple of years ago I finally wrote my biography called *Doors That Lead Nowhere*, and I guess that will be my last book. I'm finished with writing and teaching; soon life will be finished with me but that's okay; I'm eighty now, all my dreams have been realised, my wife died ten years ago, my children are adults now, the grandchildren are healthy and doing well, and I have lived a good life. Close the curtains now, give me your last ovation, and let me exit while I'm still on top. I might fart on the way out.

Sometimes I go out for a stroll, a slow walk around the block or, weather allowing, I go to the park where I feed the pigeons and have an ice cream. Some days I get lost and I go from door to door, trying my door keys on some of the doors but heading nowhere fast, hence the title of my biography. And sometimes someone steps out of the building I'm trying to get in and that someone stares at me weirdly and asks me what the fuck I'm doing and I say, "I don't fucking know."

And then I walk away silently, slowly, and I wonder where to go (but I always seem to find my way home or I ask someone for directions), and I wish I had a friend nearby or even here with me, and then I wish I was back in Cuba, but only briefly. I like this city too. In here I can get Chinese food or ice cream at any given time of the day. Which I don't. But I can.

Last time I went to Cuba I went to the Colon Cemetery to see José's grave, and I remembered our last ever talk, around 1969 or 1970, or probably around New Year's Eve 1969 or sometime nearby, and we spoke about Cuban poetry, Virgilio Piñera, Nivaria Tejera, Mariano Brull, and José told me that Cuban poetry was what you found at the end of a rainbow, and I wanted to ask him what do we find at the end of a rainbow but instead I just nodded or mumbled, maybe both, and afterwards I told him I wanted to write a novel about the apocalypse because poetry was taking me nowhere and I had bills to pay, and José looked at me as if I had offended him or broken some pact made amongst poets. But, nevertheless, offended or not, he told me about a novel he had read called *The Last Man*, written by Mary Shelley, the author of *Frankenstein*, and I told him I had never heard about it, never mind read it, and he told me the book was okay, not as good as *Frankenstein* but okay, and then I told him about a book called *The Purple Cloud*, written by someone called M. P. Shiel, a writer unknown to him, and I asked, "In case of an apocalypse, who do you think would survive, assuming there were survivors?"

"Probably a few tramps," he said.

"Why do you say that?"

"Because some tramps that I know or have seen around our area are made of sterner stuff than the normal human being and they can survive anything."

That was the last talk we ever had and I never wrote my apocalyptic novel as I was too busy writing crime novels instead, similar to the ones that Robert B. Parker wrote. The moment I swapped crime novels for poetry, I was too embarrassed to call José, and then he died, aged sixty-five my dear old friend, and others died too, so many people that I knew in Cuba, and time moved so terribly slowly, but I had my family by my side, had a few bestsellers, and made some money, so I really can't complain.

A man that I've never seen before steps out of the building and I go inside before he shuts the door behind him. He gives me a quick glance but then ignores poor old me.

Once I'm inside the building, I feel a bit lost and when someone steps out of the lift I ask, "Where am I?"

"Earth," he says.

Maybe I'm not so lost.

FRIDAY 3RD MAY 2013

On the way to nowhere…
Or to my local *Starbucks*.
I saw three lads on their second round of beers,
This was only 9:10 a.m.
Way too early for a first round,
Never mind a second round.
I saw the nerd and his girlfriend stepping out of the games shop.
Carrying under their arms two bags filled with used games.
The nerd turned to his girlfriend and said, "I fancy pizza for breakfast."
"Yeah, me too," she replied.
Needless to say, they're overweight.
I saw the charity workers chain smoking while praising the weather.
The skinny girl turned to me and smiled.
She was missing her front teeth.
I didn't smile back even though I've got all my teeth.

I saw and I heard-

At *Starbucks* I saw the pretty gay Chinese guy typing something on his laptop.
Next to him there was a copy of a book by Nathan Englander, a pack of cigarettes, and an iPhone.
I saw the Asian girl studying hard for her exams while drinking a hot chocolate.
I ordered a filtered coffee and I sat by the window so that I could watch the world go by.
Women of all shapes and sizes and races walked past the window.
Men too but I only paid attention to the women.
Sipping my coffee slowly,
I dreamt of home,
Only to realise that this place is home now.
A person changes home so many times,
Either in pursuit of a dream or stability,
Or both,
And sometimes, when one is finally stabilised,

His mind is still searching for something,
Not realising that the search is over.

At *Cocoa Caffè* I saw that they sell something called Cappachilo;
What the hell is that?
I didn't order one.
I'll stick to normal coffee.
I heard an old couple talking about the end of the world,
And I wondered if they were talking about the end of their world
Or our world.

On the way home a young couple walked past me,
Their skin covered in tattoos.
How will they look like decades from now?
What will they feel once they see their wrinkled skin covered in tattoos?
Pride or regret?
But life is short;
Live yours slowly and enjoy it.

When I got home,
I sat down and wrote this.
Afterwards I went to be bed and had a nap.
I dreamt of nothing,
Or maybe I dreamt of something
And forgot what I dreamt of.

THE SPOILED ONE

The pretty blonde standing by the counter is smiling at me. She's waiting on her cappuccino and she has recognised me. I pay for my order and then I move closer to her and wait for my drink. I'm in Victoria station, London. The station is crowded. Yoko is at some gallery in Soho getting ready for a show and I'm heading to Clapham Junction to see my brother Julian. He's been living in London for the last three years, working as a barman while squandering away the inheritance left to us by our parents. Five hundred thousand dollars isn't a lot in the hands of Julian. Before London he was in Berlin for a year or so. Before Berlin he was in Thailand. Before that I didn't hear from him for close to five months or even more. Once our mother was buried and the inheritance split between us both, he quit his job and went off to the Far East. I didn't come to London deliberately to see him. Yoko had to come here for a show and I decided to come too, and then I thought, "What the heck? I might as well go and see how Julian is doing."

The pretty blonde grabs her drink and takes a seat next to the door. She takes a book out of her bag, *Relative Stranger: A Life After Death* by Mary Loudon, and she opens the book even before she touches her drink. As for me, I carry my drink with me outside just so I can smoke a cigarette.

Lately, since she quit smoking, Yoko has been giving me grief and asking me to quit smoking too, and now I rarely smoke when I'm around her.

The heat wave is uncomfortable. I came to London expecting to see grey skies and lots of rain and I got sun instead. Apparently, today, Thursday July 18th 2013, is one of England's hottest days in decades. Just great.

I'm not a big fan of hot weather. I like the rain, a bit of wind, too, and even a bit of snow.

Riding on the underground I try to concentrate on the book that I'm reading, a copy of *A French Novel* by Frédéric Beigbeder which my agent got me. Maybe he got the book from Frédéric's agent. But as I read a few sentences of *A French Novel* my mind starts to wander off, travelling slowly back in time, back to the past, and memories I thought were forgotten become once more so clear. As the train stops for a few seconds at the next station, and then departs and heads to the next stop, the memories of my childhood and teenager years' flash past me, and, as expected, my brother Julian is such a big part of those memories, but sad to say the memories I have of him aren't fond memories. Even as a child he was a bit lazy, very spoiled indeed, especially by our mother who weakened every time Julian cried and asked for something. And afterwards he cried even more and asked for a lot more, and poor mother always complied with his wishes.

As a teenager he was even worse, always demanding a lot from everyone, including me, certainly from his girlfriends, and when he didn't get what he wanted he would sulk and stop talking to everyone. He failed at a lot of things, not because he couldn't do them but because he didn't try hard enough as he always expected everything to fall in his lap. And it did fall in his lap; a good inheritance left to us both by our parents, but while I bought a house and saved the rest wisely, Julian went off in search of the largest party ever. But every party must end and the way Julian lives his life, soon, too, his money will come to an end.

I see four copies of Brown's *Inferno* in front of me as four people devour its pages intensively, looking as if they are reading the works of Plato. Surprisingly, or maybe not, I also see someone reading Dante's *Inferno*.

I have put my book aside as I relive the past, and so lost am I in my thoughts I almost miss my stop.

I step out of the train feeling a bit tired, the memories slowly slipping away as I make my way towards Julian's place. Outside it is still hot, the park near the station is filled with people sunbathing, reading, relaxing, enjoying these rare moments of sunshine. The heat makes us feel a bit lazy and all we want to do is take it easy.

Julian knows I'm coming to see him. I emailed him a couple of days ago to tell him about my visit. At the moment he's living alone. He told me so on his last email. Living alone, working as a barman, and doing who knows what? His life nowadays is a mystery to me.

Julian has forgotten how rough our ancestors had it when they first came to America and he takes it all for granted. When our grandfather arrived in America in 1900, still a teenager, he had to start from scratch, peddle from door to door just to make a living, walk endlessly for hours and hours until he got blisters on his feet. And even then he still kept on peddling, our grandfather and other Jews too, all searching for a better way of life in America. Our great-grandfather taught the value of hard work to our grandfather, who in turn taught it to our father, who in turn taught it to us. But Julian paid no attention to what our father had to teach him. Julian had more important matters in his mind, like rock music, drugs, the poetry of Ginsberg, the writing of Burroughs, girls, alcohol, Led Zeppelin, Van Halen, and anything that didn't include any kind of work.

At school I was a bit of a nerd, not a cool guy for Julian to hang out with, but as I got older and my looks improved, my brother felt a bit competitive towards me, and once in a while he would aim a couple of punches at me just to remind me who the big brother was.

I ignored him.

I guess I got my revenge when my first book came out, the appropriately named *Revenge of the Nerd*. The book was a bestseller, selling half a million copies in the States alone, and the first thing Julian told me after the book was out was, "What a waste of paper. I can't believe people like that rubbish."

That was the sound of jealousy and defeat speaking, a sound that meant nothing to me, a sound that was soundless. Thinking about him now – and about the past - makes me want to turn around and walk away, leave him alone with his jealousy and laziness, but he's my brother, my flesh and blood, and I know that our parents would like me to keep an eye on him and give him some kind of advice, but no matter what I or anyone else says, Julian won't listen to it and he will do as he pleases, just as he always has done.

Up on a tree, crows stare absentmindedly at the people in the park. A little boy drops his ice cream on the grass and then, without his parents noticing it, he picks it up and keeps on licking. The literature lovers lie on the grass, sit on a bench, lean against trees, and I see the usual suspects on display; Nabokov, Amis, even Dickens, and a few *new* names, too; Tao Lin, Adelle Waldman, Colum McCann. Dan Brown, too. His new book is everywhere.

I walk slowly along the park, my mind here and somewhere else too, and I find myself missing New York, Central Park, the village, faces and places, but in a few hours' time I'll be with Yoko, kissing her, making love to her, and in a weeks' time we'll be in Tokyo to see her family, where I'll also give an interview to a magazine, and then it's back to the Big Apple. But for now let me enjoy these days in London.

In the park everyone is worshiping the sun, their bodies red or slightly red, the skin a bit damaged. Some bodies are orange, fake tans on display, a normal sight these days, a sign of vanity, of despair; despairing to be someone else people ignore the signs and the warnings and they use and abuse the suntan beds until their bodies can no longer take the abuse. But by then it's too late and the skin will be permanently damaged. But look who's talking; me, the smoker whose lungs want a rest from all the smoking.

Two days ago I met a strange looking woman at a party, her skin tanned to the maximum, her gigantic, fake breasts almost on display, her hair fake, too, same as her lips, her nails, her face, even her personality. She told me she was a writer too: "A famous one," she said, almost implying that she was as good as Dickens, and I simply nodded, and then she told me that she was also a supermodel and a reality TV star, and I thought, "She's everything yet she's nothing."

Her subject was, "Me, me, me."

Needless to say, she was so boring and superficial.

Pointless to say, I left her on her own and walked away.

Last year I was invited to be in a movie. Both the director and screenwriter are good friends of mine, but I declined the invitation and said, "I can't act."

The director of the movie said, "Nowadays hardly anyone can."

Nevertheless, I still said no.

Julian's curly hair is slowly leaving his head, leaving behind only a few traces of its existence. Weight wise he looks the same. He seems pleased to see me and shakes my hand vigorously. The smile on his face seems genuine too.

His place is small; a living room and kitchen combined together, two small rooms, one of which he uses as an office although I don't even know why he needs an office. He tells me the place is his; he bought it and that's good news. I'm glad he's spending some of his money wisely. On his old looking sofa a coffee-stained copy of *Beijing Coma* by Ma Jian lies open halfway, an ashtray filled with cigarette butts keeping the book open, Ma Jian being a writer whose previous works I enjoyed but I still haven't read this book of his and I know that he has a new one out called *The Dark Road*. Too many books by too many good writers come out almost every single week and a person finds it hard to keep up with them all.

Newspaper cuts lie on top of his small coffee table. A quick glance at it and I see that the newspaper cuts are all about suicide victims. Julian sees me staring at it and says, "There used to be a lot of suicide clubs online where people would chat and then meet up, which in a way was good because it meant that none of these lonely people had to die alone, but now most of those sites have been closed and more depressed people are dying alone."

"Maybe they need some kind of help and guidance instead of a suicide club," I say, wondering why we're having such a morbid talk.

"What kind of help? Prozac? Antidepressants? Medication? Some psychiatric telling them what to do and how to live their lives? Maybe they don't want –and don't need- that."

"But isn't suicide a bit dramatic?"

"Dramatic? Isn't living in pain dramatic too?" he says.

A large canvas displaying New York takes centre stage in a wall of his living room, a canvas available at IKEA, and the rest of his furniture also seems to have been bought there, including the small bookcases where I recognise some of the titles straight away; *The Kingdom of Auschwitz* by Otto Friedrich and *Memory of Childhood Trauma: A Clinician's Guide to the Literature*, but while I recognise the names of some of the authors; Paul Auster, Malcolm Gladwell, Sam Lipsyte, for some reason the titles of their books seem vaguely blurry.

"What if there was someone out there that could guide these people, have them all together in a group of four, to make sure they never had to die alone?" says Julian while suddenly my eyes feel a bit tired, in need of rest. I've been feeling like this for quite a while and Yoko has told me to go to the opticians, but my vain self doesn't want to wear glasses. Well, it looks as if I won't have a choice in the matter.

I try to change the subject; why mention death and suicide at a time like this, at a time when two brothers who haven't seen each other in a long time are reunited?

I ask him how he is, what has he been up to for the last few years, and he tells me about drugs and prostitutes, gambling and trannies in East Asia, crossdressing and more gambling, and he also tells me how he blew most of his inheritance before arriving in London, and after buying this flat and some furniture, he was almost broke, but, thankfully, he found a job in a bar straight away, and he's also going to rent the spare room to *a gorgeous student to make some extra cash.*

Listening to Julian talk is like listening to an old record from long time ago, a record I never liked. I'm not asking him to be perfect; G-d knows how much I've sinned, but at least try to live a decent life.

"Drugs aren't bad, man. I don't do them out there in the open. I do it here, at my place, and then I pass out and dream. There's nothing wrong with that," he says, sounding like a student that gets told he's wrong but keeps doing the same mistake over and over again. He's a spoiled man that fails to learn from his mistakes and he'll have to learn the hard way, as many of us do.

I stay there for twenty minutes or so. There's not much to talk about and the subjects that Julian brings into the conversation –drugs, suicide, madness- are things I know nothing of, so, with relief from both sides, we shake hands and I head back to the hotel.

Once I'm standing outside, I discover that I don't feel like smoking anymore, or so I think, but five minutes later, once I buy a coffee from a place nearby, I light a cigarette and I sit on a bench in the park.

A week later I arrive in Tokyo with Yoko and we discover, to our dismay, that her younger brother has committed collective suicide with three other strangers. The first thing that comes to my mind is, "At least he didn't die alone," but then I come to the conclusion that he did die alone even though he was with others.

Back at my place in Upper West Side I read a few pages of a book that belongs to Yoko; something called *And So Can You* by Mitsuyo Ohira, I listen to *Look Forward to Failure* by The Ataris – and that inspires me to start working on a new book which I will call *Looking Forward to Success.*

Two days spent entirely working on the book I change its title to *Tokyo/Nowhere.* Two weeks after that I find out I have cancer and not so long to live. Luckily I manage to finish the book, a novella once it's typed, and I know that no matter what I won't die alone because I have someone I love by my side...

(Taken from John Sparks's diary)

55

INEBRIATED BRAIN

His name was Sam; Sam something - I can't remember his last name - and he used to be a great musician. He played the piano. His heroes were Oscar Peterson and Bill Evans, and he was well-known all over his town, and other places, too. People came from all over the place to listen to him play, and at the end of every show everyone would buy him a drink. That's what brought him down; the booze, the constant drinking, the never-ending parties. He fell in love, got married, had a daughter, but he kept on drinking, more and more every day, and soon enough hardly a day went by when he was sober. The booze drove him towards other women, and at first his wife tried to look the other way, and afterwards she tried to save the marriage, but her efforts turned to nothing and the marriage came to an end. Sam remained in his town but his wife and daughter moved out, to Faro at first, and then to Lisbon. When I met him it had been years since he last had seen his daughter and he now looked a mess. Only fifty-five years old, he looked to be around seventy, all because of his drinking addiction, and the talent he once possessed was now forgotten, the love of music replaced by the drinking addiction. At night, alone by then, in his small, smelly, rented room, many nights Sam found it hard to fall asleep, not because of sadness but due to the state of his body and mind, all because of the booze. And some nights, feeling too lazy to leave his room and go downstairs to use the bathroom, he would get up, shit in a plastic bag, and then throw the bag towards someone's roof. And then in the morning someone would come ringing the doorbell at the house where I lived, and that someone would complain about Sam. This went on for years and Sam would say it wasn't him; he would cry injustice to the skies, but a few days later he would be doing the same thing again. He was lost, so lost he didn't even know that he was lost, but the people around him, instead of helping him find his way, only helped him to sink lower. With time his health started to deteriorate and one day he had to be hospitalized because his liver no longer could take all that drinking. The doctor told Sam he didn't had long to live, asked him if he had any family to pay for the medical bill, and then someone managed to contact his daughter who said she didn't want a thing to do with her father. Who could blame her since he never helped the poor girl with anything?

A few days after he had gone to hospital Sam died; his poor fragile thin body no longer was able to fight against the addiction that had crippled him. I don't know who paid for his funeral but I know that none of his drinking buddies went to it.

This morning, walking down the road, as I headed towards the city centre, dead flowers on the street, stepped on by the feet of the drunken generation, pavements filled with broken bottles, discarded food, too, I thought of Sam, years after he had died. He left nothing behind but memories of a helpless inebriated character, and I bet that not even his daughter thinks of him now.

THE POET AND ME

I once shared a studio with a poet while living in London. I slept on the sofa and the poet slept in a small bed, and we shared the kitchen, bathroom, and the poet's books. His name was complicated so I just called him De, which a lot of his friends also did. The place where we lived was in Ealing Broadway, a nice area of London, and the studio belonged to the poet's parents, but they had moved to Essex and left the studio to him. He had long shelves that went all the way to the ceiling filled with books of poetry, psychology, fiction, and lots of biographies and memoirs. There were also a few books about Buddhism and about stars in the shelves but I never touched those.

The poet was a pain in the ass, always quoting poetry, poem after poem, and I would ask, "Is that one of yours?" and he would reply, "No, this is *The Sisters of Charity* by Jean Arthur Rimbaud."

Nobody that I know ever calls Rimbaud by his full name, but, as I said, the poet was a pain in the ass and a bit of a snob, too, but he was also a good cook and every Sunday he would cook lunch for us.

A day would go by, and I would be on the sofa reading Henry Miller or Philip Roth, and the poet would quote another poem, and then I would ask, "Is that one of yours?" and he would say, "No, this is David Gasgoyne."

Another day would go by, another poem would be read by the poet; I would ask the usual question: "Is that one of yours?" and the poet would say, "No. This is Douglas Dunn."

One day he read a poem by T. S. Eliot; I asked the question, got the usual answer, and then, exasperated because of the poet, I asked, "Do you even write poems?"

Shyly, he replied, "I'm trying."

Feeling calmer, I said, "Well, if you haven't written any poem yet, you shouldn't call yourself a poet."

A few days went by where the poet didn't read a single poem out loud, but then one day, early in the morning, this on a Sunday, just as I was getting ready to go to the café to meet another friend for a chat, De read a poem to which I paid hardly any attention, and afterwards I asked, "Who wrote that one?"

"I did," he replied, and his answer was followed by a huge smile.

"It's quite good," I said, even though I couldn't remember what he had read.

A couple of days went by and he read another poem. I said, "Excellent poem. Congratulations."

"Oh, I didn't write it. Verlaine did."

He kept reading poem after poem throughout the months that I was there with him, but, apart from that one poem, he never wrote another poem.

Still, he had written one so I guess he could call himself a poet.

The reason why I'm now writing about De it's because only a few days ago I read a short story of his in a magazine, a story called *My Anal Lover*, and I was surprised and happy to see his name in a magazine; his name and also a small picture of him standing outside a museum. I went on Facebook and searched for his name, found him straight away, and then I sent him a message. Now I'm waiting on a reply.

My anal lover

Memories are funny; they vanish for a while, and just when you thought a face, a name, a memory was forgotten, it suddenly comes back to you, not to haunt you but to remind you of what was left behind.

Walking down the avenue last Wednesday morning on the way to work, headphones on, Violent Femmes playing on my MP3, the cold wind on my face and my body still half asleep, in need of some caffeine to wake me up, a name from the past came to my mind, a name that I had almost forgotten, a name and dare I say a sexual secret that only me and Corrine, that name from the past, know about.

More than a decade ago I was living in Neasden, doing absolutely nothing with my life apart from working and spending my wages on nothing that could satisfy me. To be fair, the wages that I earned working as a barman barely allowed me to live a decent life, but whatever little I had left once I paid my bills, I would spend it on books, takeaway food, cigarettes and booze. I lived only for the moment, never thinking about tomorrow. Back then I read a lot of crime novels, especially the works of Eric Lustbader, Trevanian, Marc Olden, and Richard La Plante among others, and I watched a lot of action movies by the likes of Steven Seagal, Van Damme, and so many others, and now I don't even bother to watch any of those movies anymore. This was the '90s, a decade that went too slow for me and where I wrote absolutely nothing apart from a few short stories. I wasn't lazy back then. I was VERY lazy when it came to writing, but I did read like a madman. On Friday nights, when most of the tenants in the house where I lived were out, I would be alone in the kitchen, reading and smoking, probably drinking a beer, too. I always worked on Fridays but I finished around 11 p.m., and less than fifteen minutes later, I would be at home since I didn't live too far from where I worked. The house where I lived was owned by an English man and an Italian woman, and they were good landlords. Six other people lived in the house; three women and three men, and one of the men, Old Joe, wasn't that sane anymore so we hardly ever saw him. If you ever left any leftovers around the kitchen, Joe would come into the kitchen and eat it, and then he would act as if nothing had happened when we asked who had eaten our food. The guy was demented and he had that odd smell that some old people tend to have. What is that smell anyway? Never mind; I'll find out one day when I reach Joe's age.

On Fridays I would be the only person in the house along with Joe, but he hardly ever left his room so I had the whole house for myself. Corrine had changed jobs and she was spending Fridays at home too, but she would usually be in her room studying for her exams and I would hardly see her, and whenever we happened to bump into one another at home we would hardly say a word to each other. One Friday night, minutes after I had just arrived from work, Corrine came into the kitchen and asked me for a lighter. There were a couple of lighters in one of the drawers, not to mention a few boxes of matches, too, but nevertheless I reached into my pocket and lit her cigarette. At the time I was trying to write a movie called *Slick* about a professional hitman that decides to quit after one last job and I kept writing it and rewriting it until I finally couldn't bear to stare at it, so after years of having the idea in my head – and a few pages written down - I put the movie aside once and for all. I lacked the discipline needed to become a writer. Stability, too, because that's needed for the mind to be at rest. A hundred stories were playing in my head, but I was like Henry Miller in Brooklyn, before he left for Paris where he wrote the classics *Tropic of Capricorn* and *Tropic of Cancer*, and I couldn't stand still to write a single story.

Corrine sat by my side and asked me what I was writing and I told her about the story for *Slick*. She said it sounded good, asked me how far I was into it and had I written anything else, and me, to show off a bit, told her I had written plenty of short stories, a few poems, too, but was now trying to write a proper movie. If I sounded naïve that's because I was indeed naïve, but Corrine didn't seem to mind. Little did I know that she had something else in mind. I finished drinking a bottle of Bud, took a last puff on the cigarette, and then I got up and took another bottle of Bud from the fridge. I asked Corrine if she wanted one but she told me she didn't drink alcohol. I sat down, expecting her to leave and go back to her room and her studies, but she stayed where she was, standing by the sink, watching me, and that made me a bit uncomfortable, but I said nothing.

She asked, "How come you're here alone?"

"I work on Fridays until 11 p.m. and after work I just want to rest and have some time for myself. I'm not really a partygoer," I said.

"Neither am I," she said.

I wanted to read a bit, or maybe keep on writing, but her presence made me feel a bit uncomfortable so I kept on drinking while staring at the blank pages in front of me. Corrine turned around and took a soft drink from the fridge, swallowed some of it, and then turned to me and said, "Would you like to come to my room and watch a movie?"

Those words took me by surprise but I was excited and the first thing that came to my mind was sex. And I sure needed it since it had been close to one year since I last had wetted my brush. My heart beating faster than usual, I followed Corrine upstairs. She lived on the first floor, her bedroom being next to mine, and, like me, she too read loads, but her taste in reading was more serious than mine. She read Balzac, Zola, and even Proust at a time when I still didn't know who the great narrator of time was, and she also read Dante and Yeats and so many other authors that I hadn't yet bother to read. Her room was as big as mine, but she had a desk filled with books, an old computer on top of the desk, notepads filled with notes for her studies, drawings that she made whenever she went to a museum, but I wasn't there to talk about books. I sat nervously on her bed, right next to her, as there was only one chair available and there were some books on top of it. The movie she chose for us to watch was *The Last Seduction*, a title most appropriate for that night, and barely ten minutes into the movie, when she saw that I was too shy to make a move, she took control of the situation, just like Linda Fiorentino did in the movie that we were watching, and she touched one of my legs, letting me know where the night was heading to, and that was the direction that I wanted it to take. My penis obeyed the movements of her hand straight away. As I've said, it had been ages since I last had sex with anyone and my penis had been on a long diet, a diet that was coming to an end. Before I knew it we were kissing, the movie playing for no one, and my hands started to remove her shirt while her hands started to remove my trousers. She went down on me, too fast I must say, and she looked as if she was starving for it too, but as I said, it had been too long since I last had sex and I didn't want to spoil it by coming too quickly so I gently grabbed her head and pulled her away. She then guided my head – and tongue - towards her vagina, and she spread her legs wide open while I satisfied her. My penis was dying to get in, feed itself, eat the vagina and let it all out, and when I was getting ready to enter, she told me to wait and then put a condom on me. Then she put some cream on the condom and said, "Only anally as I want to stay a virgin until I marry."

Whoa! Forbidden territory. The black hole that I hadn't yet dared to enter.

I hesitated.

That was a first and I wasn't sure if I could go ahead with it, but my penis was telling me to go in: "A hole is a hole and I need to eat," it said to me and I obeyed the penis. It was like that episode of Seinfeld, *The Nose Job*, where Jerry is having doubts about his relationship with Tawny Kitaen and his brain has a chess match with his penis.

I went in, or should I say I slide it in easily due to the cream, and Corrine let out a low scream of pleasure.

When it was all over and done with, we lay in bed together, and I was hoping to spend the night with her because I sure needed some company, but she said it would be better if I went back to my bedroom because she didn't want anyone in the house to know that we had done it. I left her room feeling a bit rejected, but happy, too, because I had done it.

On Saturday and Sunday I didn't see her because she went away, probably to visit her folks, and on Monday I only saw her briefly, but there were other people in the house and we didn't even speak to one another. I kept looking at her to see if she would acknowledge me but nothing, not even a quick glance towards me. I thought that night would be forgotten but on the next Friday, when I was in the kitchen reading Poe, cigarette burning in the ashtray, a half empty glass of whisky on the side, ice melting away slowly, Corrine came in the house and walked straight into the kitchen. This time she said hi and smiled at me, and I knew we were on again. We didn't waste time with small talk. I followed her into her bedroom and we repeated the process. She was my Friday girl, my anal lover, and this went on for close to three months. Not once did we go out or do a thing apart from sex, which was fine by me as I was completely on my own in London and it was good to have that company for one day a week, and the sex was good too, but looking back I realise that we used one another to obtain what we wanted, which was nothing but a good time.

One day I returned home, this during summer, and I found out that she was gone. Just then I felt really low, loner than before, but months later I also moved out, found someone else, if only for a few months, and I quickly forgot about my anal lover.

Years went by without me ever thinking about Corrine until that Wednesday morning, and on that afternoon I went on Facebook to see if I could find her, which I did, and I saw that she's now married, a bit chubbier than before, older too since age catches up with all of us, and I felt tempted to send her a message but what would be the point of it?

She has probably forgotten all about me -and I'm fine with it- and I know that we might never meet again. And what would we say if we did meet? How would we react?

Some faces are better forgotten, as are some memories.

LOST & FOUND
(& LEFT BEHIND)

On the way to work I saw a lost glove on the floor,
A pair of shoes left behind, outside a pub,
Pink in colour,
High heels.
I wonder how she walked home.
Maybe she got a cab…
I saw a scarf a meter away from where the shoes were,
A furry hat even further away,
Followed by another hat not that far from where the furry one was.
Was she naked?
Did she had two heads or did the other hat belong to a friend of hers?
Or maybe they belonged to someone else.

I saw children's toys, too,
Abandoned, lost, or simply left behind.
I saw them all but I picked up none.
If I took home everything that I found, I could open a shop.
Or my neighbours and landlord would think that I've gone crazy.

NOTHING LEFT

From my window I saw you crying on your own.

Night after night, tear after tear, I saw you and I waited.

I was thinking of jumping but I waited just a bit longer because I wanted to see how deep your pain was. Most of all, I wanted to see if you would join me.

And so I waited before approaching you, and afterwards we spoke, and you told me your dreams, and they were my nightmares, and we could see that there was nothing left in this world for us.

We held hands before jumping, and for a moment I felt like I was flying.

(Suicide note, left behind in someone's bag)

JERUSALEM

At a café drinking and writing, a book of Jewish-American literature by my side: Abraham Cahan, Leo Rosten, Emma Lazarus, Bret Harte, Karl Shapiro, and so many others; all of them are in the book, and a stranger asks, "Where are you from?"

An unexpected question, especially when it comes from the mouth of a stranger, and it takes me seconds to reply, and what can I say?

I tell him the truth…

I'm the son of emigrants, and so is he.

He tells me a sad tale with a few happy moments in between, a tale I've heard so often from different mouths, differing from mine in places and faces.

Once outside, we shake hands, making no promises to meet again.

A dream is waiting for us, a dream and a name: Jerusalem.

He's heading there.

I've just returned.

Maybe we'll meet there again someday.

THE JEALOUS ONE

The doors of the café make a creaking noise. Someone has just walked in. Julio is smoking a Marlboro Lights which he took from his wife's bag this morning; a packet with four cigarettes in it, and she said it was okay because she had another packet in her coat. Then he told her he was going to the café to meet Ashok and he blew her a kiss, and she said, "Come here and give me a proper kiss."

Outside, little drops of rain were falling softly from the sky and his wife Corrine told him to take an umbrella with him, and after giving her a proper kiss, he said, "Okay."

And now he's in the café staring vaguely at a book by Mehdi Charef called *Tea in the Harem* while waiting for his friend Ashok to arrive. And the sun is out but he still has to carry the umbrella with him. He remembers one time when he went out and took an umbrella with him, but then, fed up with carrying the damn thing everywhere, he deliberately left it at a café, and hours later the rain came falling down heavily in the city and he had to go and buy another umbrella while he was still outside.

He flicks through the pages slowly, his mind absent, halfway between a dream and an idea, a sure sign for inspiration, and then he hears a familiar voice ordering a double espresso, a voice he hasn't heard in a long time, but that same voice is still recorded somewhere in his brain, a voice from the past. Its 10 a.m., a quiet day at the café, quiet for now but once the office workers leave for lunch the place will be full.

At first Julio ignores the voice but then he looks up and he sees the face of his old friend Elvis, a young man named after the King of rock n' roll, a man who years ago was Julio's best friend but now they don't even say hello to one another. Elvis sees him too but looks the other way, and then, irritated and annoyed, upset for having seen Julio, he goes back to the counter and tells the barista to put his double espresso in a takeaway cup, and once the barista complies with his wish, Elvis walks away, still annoyed and irritated.

The sound of Kraftwerk is coming out from the hidden speakers, spoons are stirring the coffee and the sugar and the milk, the barista is putting his art into practice, and Julio sees Elvis drinking the coffee outside, down the throat it goes in one go, too fast, no time to enjoy it properly, and then he watches his old friend walk away at a fast pace, looking as if he's trying to outrun some kind of danger.

A cab stops in front of the café and seconds later a man steps out of it. It is Ashok, a man who is now Julio's best friend, the position held by Elvis a few years ago. Ashok carries under his arms a Samsung Chromebook. Nowadays, wherever he goes, he carries the machine with him at all times. He lives in the Cloud, Cyberspace, the iLife, his existence on Facebook for everyone to see, the tweets up there for his 122 followers to read, that is if they bother with it. As for Julio, he's the opposite of Ashok. He's hardly ever online, never tweets, and has less than thirty friends on Facebook. He had thirty until this morning but two of them unfriended him, all because he doesn't share a lot online, never hits the like button, never writes any comments but he's fine with it.

Ashok orders a large black coffee, cold milk on the side, and a cheese sandwich, too, toasted, and after he sits down he extracts a book from his laptop bag, an old copy of *The Rebels* by Sándor Márai, and hands it over to Julio.

At the moment Márai is Julio's favourite writer. So far he has read *Embers, Casanova in Bolzano, Esther's Inheritance*, the already mentioned *The Rebels*, and he's waiting for *Memoir of Hungary* to arrive in the mail. He goes through phases where he has a new favourite author. Not so long ago Bolaño was his favourite author and Bolaño held that position far longer than any author, even longer than Haruki Murakami, but now Sándor Márai is the main man. Or the main author. Years ago Susan Sontag was his favourite author but he hasn't read her in years. As for Ashok, Bolaño is his favourite author and he reads *The Savage Detectives* every year, devouring it as if it were some kind of sacred scriptures. He also loves to read – and re-read - the works of Anne Roiphe and Joan Didion.

Julio tells Ashok about Elvis, who still happens to be friends with Ashok, and Ashok tells Julio not to worry about him.

"I'm not worried. I just find the whole thing silly," says Julio.

"Jealousy is a hard thing to let go," says Ashok while trying to get connected to the internet. He logs on, and then talks, eats, drinks and types without taking his eyes of the small screen in front of him. He tweets: *at the café, chilling out*. He takes a picture of the café, then posts an entry on Facebook, adding the picture that he just took, and he writes: *at the café, chilling out, enjoying the day.* Minutes later he posts another entry on Facebook: *trying to write a new poem, something to do with apples and cars.* He tweets: *Apples and cars. Yummy and yes!*

A woman enters the café, scans the place with her big brown eyes, and when she sees Julio she waves at him. He waves back at her; at Sola, a poetess from Nigeria that has been living in London since she was two. She orders a sandwich, a medium black coffee, no milk on the side, no sugar either, and she asks Julio if he wants something, and he thanks her and says no. Sola then joins both men and tells Ashok to get offline for a few minutes. He looks at her and she shoots him one of her pretty, large smiles, which makes him smile too and, reluctantly, he turns the computer off. She shows Julio a copy of a book she got yesterday from Waterstones; Milo de Angelis's *Theme of Farewell and After-Poems*, and Julio browses slowly through the book, reading a couple of poems at random. Afterwards they talk about a poetry reading event that the three of them are going to attend, and thirty minutes later Sola leaves the café and heads to the library where she works four hours every afternoon. Julio checks the time and says, "Damn it, I've been here for more than two hours!"

Ashok says, "Don't worry about it. It's not like the world is going to end because of it. Anyway, where's Corrine?"

"She's at work," says Julio.

Corrine is his wife; pretty Corrine, 26-years-old, Cambridge-born, a Cambridge graduate, and also the reason why Elvis has stopped talking with Julio, not because he loved her or anything like that, but because he felt envy towards his friend's good fortune.

Before Julio met Corrine his life was heading nowhere. He had been working for the last two years on a novel while working as a labourer for a construction firm, and he was renting a tiny room in Hackney, not that far from where Elvis lived. But Elvis lived in a big house with his parents, in a house where everything was handed to him on a plate, and, secretly, he loved seeing Julio's life in a mess because it made his life look so good. They had been friends at school, but then lost touch for a couple of years before meeting again in college. And while Elvis kept on studying Julio had to quit his studies and find a job because his parents were too lost in drugs to have the time to help him with anything.

Lacking studies, Julio got a job as a general labourer, a job he absolutely hated and where he had to put up with a lot of crap, but the money was good and he managed to rent a small room in a good house. His mother died five years ago; drugs, AIDS, maybe a mixture of both, and his father died shortly afterwards from the same causes, maybe, maybe not. By then Julio was too busy trying to survive to even pay attention to what his parents were doing to themselves. At first he tried to help them but his father tried to beat him up when Julio offered him help and his mother wanted him to steal for them so that they could afford to buy more drugs.

During that time Elvis was always by Julio's side, listening to him complain about his life, the lack of good parents, how shit his job was, how he wished he could go back to studying and get a degree, and at night, while Julio lay in bed staring at the ceiling, Elvis played videogames until dawn.

One night Julio decided to stop feeling sorry for himself and he applied for night school. He kept that a secret from everyone, including Elvis, because he felt a bit embarrassed about it and also just in case he failed his exams. He met Ashok at night school and the two of them became friends straight away. During the week Ashok worked in two buildings as a cleaner and on the weekends he washed dishes at an Italian restaurant in Soho, cash in hand so he didn't have to pay any tax. He dreamt of becoming a bookkeeper and a poet, just like his hero Fernando Pessoa, and now he's both; a bookkeeper and a poet.

Julio had no dreams; no nightmares either which was good, but one day he read *Tropic of Cancer* followed by *Black Spring*, and afterwards he felt an urge to write a novel.

It was Ashok who introduced Julio to Corrine. She worked on the Human Resources department in one of the buildings where Ashok worked as a cleaner, and he would see her quite often reading Tomas Tranströmer or Mina Loy, or other poets that he liked, and one night he invited her to come to a poetry reading where he would be reading a couple of poems of his, and she said okay. Ashok wasn't interested in her. He just wanted her to hear/see him read. Julio was also there and that's when Ashok introduced him to Corrine. It took around ten seconds for Julio to fall in love with her. It took longer for Corrine to fall in love with him, but only five or six seconds more. They became a couple on that same week, and when Elvis saw that Julio's life was heading on the right direction he became bitter, consumed by jealousy, and he started to avoid his friend.

After six months of them going out together, Corrine said that they should share a place together instead of renting two rooms and Julio said yes straight away. Once he moved in with her, his writing started to improve, to be longer, and after a year or so his book was finished. He called it *Damaged Kingdom*. After spending a few months editing the book, he sent it to fifty agents and then waited for a reply. Little by little, he started to receive rejection after rejection, and whenever that happened, he felt a bit foolish for thinking that he would make it straight away.

One afternoon he happened to bump into Elvis just outside the library where Sola worked and he invited his friend for a drink at a nearby pub. Elvis didn't seem too keen on it and Julio found that a bit odd since they always had been good friends, or at least he thought they were good friends but maybe he had been wrong about that, and after a couple of beers and a plate of fries, Julio told him what he had been doing with his life, including the book he had written, and also about the rejections, and when Elvis heard about the rejections, he grinned and then said, "What makes you think you're a writer?"

His tone of voice was aggressive, and Julio wondered what the hell was wrong with him, why was he being so negative, so rude, so aggressive, and then he also wondered where the hell his friend had been for the last few months, why didn't he ever call him or pick up the phone or at least email him, and some sort of rage started to grow inside him, but he kept his cool and said, "Why can't I be a writer? Everyone has to start somewhere."

"Yes, but you're not a writer!" said Elvis, sounding even more aggressive, and Julio was starting to be upset, but he kept his cool and said, "Says who?"

"I say! You're not a writer! You're not an artist!" Elvis wanted to say, "You're nobody," but he held those words inside him.

"But I wrote a book so that makes me a writer," Julio said defensively.

"But it's shit!" By then Elvis's voice was getting a bit too loud and there were plenty of eyes staring at them.

"How do you know? You haven't read it," said Julio, and he was surprised of how calm he sounded.

"I'm telling you, it is shit!" and then Elvis got up and walked away, and Julio wondered what the hell had just happened.

The Irish barmaid walked over to his table, smiled, collected the dirty glasses, and then said, "Envy."

Julio looked at her and she shrugged her shoulders before walking away, and he knew she was right; his friend was jealous of him.

That same night Elvis changed his phone number and deleted Julio's email address.

As for Julio, he sat at the bar on his own for a few more minutes, still wondering why his friend was acting so childishly, and when he got home he found three rejections in the post box. Forty-seven and counting. That made him feel a bit depressed, and later on, when he told Sola and Corrine what happened between him and Elvis, Sola said, "He's the jealous one, the one who can never be happy because someone else always has something that he doesn't have."

On the next day he got another rejection, followed by another and another throughout the week, and he sent his manuscript to two other agents and started writing a sequel to *Damaged Kingdom*. He called it *Repairing the Soul*.

Julio can't remember when he finally got a positive answer; it was probably the 56th or 57th agent, but at least it was easier to find someone willing to publish the book. By then he already had finished his studies, had quit his job at the construction firm, and was doing administration work at the same place where Corrine worked, but while she worked from 9 a.m. to 5 p.m., he started at 9 a.m. and finished at 2 p.m., and afterwards he would go home and write for three straight hours, only pausing for a piss, a smoke, or a glass of water.

Damaged Kingdom came out around the time that Julio started to type *Repairing the Soul*. The book did okay in England but did even better in Norway, Denmark and France, becoming a huge bestseller in those countries.

Julio was happy. And sad, too. Sad because of the way Elvis had behaved, and one night he sent a message to his old friend on Facebook but never got a reply. On that same night Elvis blocked him from his contacts. Slowly, the jealousy was consuming Elvis.

Elvis leaves home just before 7 p.m. He takes a bus to Hammersmith and he sees one of the passengers reading an old copy of *Repairing the Soul*. The book came out less than two years ago but the hardback copy that is being held by the woman sitting in front of him looks old and damaged. By the traffic lights he sees two black teenagers singing and laughing. They look happy and Elvis smiles but then he looks at the woman reading Julio's book and the smile quickly leaves his face. Standing behind him, waiting for a free seat, a young couple are discussing the movie version of *Cloud Atlas*, and although they can't agree if the movie is bad or good, both say that Tom Hanks is one of the greatest actors ever. A few seconds go by and the man says, "But Tom isn't as good as Marlon Brando."

"Oh, please," the woman says. "Name me one good..."

Elvis never hears the rest of the sentence because he gets up and presses the buzzer as he's reaching his destination.

Ashok is standing outside a bar in Hammersmith having a chat with his friend Frank when he sees Elvis on the other side of the road waiting by the traffic lights, looking seemingly lost amongst the vast population of London.

Frank is saying, "I haven't been to Hammersmith in years. Almost every morning I catch a bus that drives past here but I can't even recall the last time I was here. Oh no, wait, I can. It was when Whitesnake released *Forevermore*. Can you believe it?"

"Yeah I can," Ashok says, a cigarette stuck between his lips.

Elvis sees them too and approaches them, and one of them says, "Hey, what's up?" and someone else says, "How you doing?" and maybe Elvis says, "Long time no see," and Frank, always the comedian, says, "Damn, you're still ugly," and Elvis laughs and says, "Look who's talking?" but deep inside he's upset.

"What are you doing here?" Ashok asks.

"The poetry reading, of course. What about you? Are you going to read some of your work?" says Elvis.

"Yes, but I'm still waiting for Julio to arrive."

"He's coming?"

"Yeah. He's reading a chapter from his new book."

Elvis excuses himself and says he has to go, and before any of the other men can say another word, he crosses the road and walks away. He goes to another bar where he drinks four shots of tequila and two pints of beer. When he goes to the bathroom he sees a leaflet on the floor, something about a BogMan. He picks it up and shoves it in his pocket, and then goes back to the bar for another beer.

"What's the name of your third book?" Frank asks.

"*Naivety and Stupidity*," says Julio.

"Shit, man, you should have called it *Virgins and Whores*," says Frank, and both men laugh, and Julio actually likes that title (but he won't use it).

Corrine tells them to keep quiet because Sola is about to go on stage. That night, once Ashok goes back to his place, Corrine and Julio go to Frank and Sola's new place, a few stops outside London.

Frank and Sola have hardly any furniture at home so they decide to set up a large tent in their living room and the four of them camp in there. They light up candles, leave the curtains open, and look at the moon while sipping red wine inside the tent.

Frank says, "This is cool."

Julio nods, Corrine smiles, and Sola wraps her arms around Frank.

In the back of his head Julio is thinking about Elvis and he hopes his old friend is alright and not alone. Julio, too, knows how it feels to be jealous of others. When he was alone and had nothing, sometimes he too felt a bit jealous of those who were happy.

On the next morning they have coffee and pancakes with syrup and strawberries'. Since it's Saturday and the weather is good, and none of them has to go to work, they go to the park and afterwards they go to IKEA to buy some furniture for Frank and Sola's place.

That same night Ashok calls Julio who is already back at his place in London.

Ashok says, "They're about to start a war!"

"Who is?" Julio asks.

Corrine is already in bed, fast asleep, while Julio is watching a movie called *Moon* with Sam Rockwell.

"Everyone!" Ashok says.

"Are you sure?"

"Yes!"

Julio stops the DVD and switches to the news.

Oh, no!

Right now he's staring at the end.

Elvis approaches the car slowly. Judith is leaning against it while smoking her last cigarette, and John and Tracey, all strangers to him, are already inside the car. The four of them are about to meet the BogMan.

WHAT I SAW

Things I've seen on the way here…

Where is here?

I saw…
A man collapsing on the floor.
People around him trying to resurrect him.
A man dying.
Shining objects in the sky moving fast along a straight line.
Two stupefied eyes staring at me while the mouth asked, "What was that?"
"Don't know," I answered.
Decades later, a shining object hovering above me. Not an aeroplane, not a drone (I think), certainly not a helicopter, but what was it?
What were those shining objects?
Does anyone have Fox Mulder's number?

I saw…
A man falling in love with a woman.
I think I was the man.
A balloon bursting and a child crying.
Another balloon bursting.
Another child crying.
And another balloon…
And a child laughing.
I guess the balloon wasn't his.

I saw…
Death.
Life.
Pain.
A man holding hands with another man.
A woman falling in love with another woman.
Another man dying while we at work wondered what was happening.
Someone tearing a book apart.

A fish that had been caught begging to be let back in the sea, his eyes pleading while the fisherman laughed.
A mother smoking while her child was coughing.
Stupid mother.

TOO GOOD

I used to greet Julie every morning when she arrived at work and she would greet me back, always with a smile on her face, a smile that was just a bit too much, a bit fake, a display of falseness, but I made nothing of it. I come to work to earn my wages, and to look after my family and buy some of the things that I want, and not to worry about how others act, but sometimes one has to stop, look around, and take some kind of action towards ignorance or else others will think of you as weak and stupid. Don't get mad towards others who ignore you; he who angers you conquers you, but pay them back on the same way too, always with a smile on your face.

One morning I was heading to the restaurant and I happened to bump into Julie. I said hello to her but she kept on walking, her eyes looking ahead, her attitude towards me one of scorn, and she acted as if I wasn't even there. I made nothing of it and I thought she was having just a bad day, but deep inside I knew what her problem was.

On the following morning, the moment she walked in through the front door, Julie put on her fake display once more, her greeting a bit over the top, and as usual I made nothing of it and greeted her too, normally, not exaggerating it, greeting her politely as I greet everyone. A few hours later I bumped into her again, this time at the café, and when I said hello to her she ignored me. I was sure I knew then what her problem was but instead of getting upset (and what would I gain from it?) I decided to ignore her too, and on the next day, when she came to work, I looked away and pretend to be busy when she said good morning to me, and then I did the same thing again when she left in the afternoon. For a week or so I ignored her greetings, and nowadays she greets me shyly while I greet her coldly. I've got nothing against her but I can't stand these people that think they're too good to speak with you only because they hold a higher position. Please, give me a break; we're all the same. Don't you clean your arse too when you go to the bathroom?

This action of Julie is nothing new; it has happened before at work, more than once, more than twice, and it will happen again, and that only shows how some people judge others by their positions and status, not just here where I work but everywhere.

Sad, isn't it?

More pathetic than sad, actually, especially now that we're looking at the end of it all, and many of us, including me, are wondering what was the point of acting so arrogantly towards others, but we only came to this conclusion because of what is about to happen, if anything happens, and if nothing happens and there's no war, we will still resort to being our old selves. Whichever way we look the human race is doomed because of their behaviour. Blow it all, I say, blow this shitty planet to bits. We don't deserve it.

A PORTRAIT
OF THE END

The power went off and we were left in the dark.

Our iPods, iPhones, iPads, MacBooks were completely dead.

The Pixies – and Bieber - became nothing but a memory as our expensive gadgets quickly turned into junk.

The water running from the tap was dirty and brown, undrinkable and smelly.

No TV, no radio, no electricity, so we read our old books and whatever else we could find on paper.

We ate the meat and the cheese in the fridge as quickly as we could before it all went off.

Night came and we waited for salvation.

For good news, a miracle, but what good was that?

Our leaders were living underground, maybe at Denver Airport, still connected, those selfish buggers, their iGadgets still working, their food fresh and eatable, their water clean and drinkable.

As for us, the people, we survived on canned food and bottled water, followed by what else we could find.

Some people went crazy, panicked, and committed suicide just as they were running out of food.

Like others, I left my house and I went out in pursuit of food.

Around me I saw dead bodies, their flesh dried up in the sun, and I saw rats being burnt by survivors. Their meat smelled good and I thought about Stallone and *Demolition Man*, and I kept on walking, my legs aching and my mouth dry.

Miles away I found food, nicely packed in cans, bottled water, fizzy drinks, and books that hadn't been read in ages.

I ate, drank, read Proust and Poe, got bored quickly, played with Lego, read *Green Lantern* and the *Fantastic Four*, followed by *Flash* and *The Hardy Boys*, and then I slept for hours.

The end of days had arrived.

The sun was dying and the people were melting away slowly.

I woke up in the morning, covered in sweat.

I missed coffee and toast, family and friends, and so much more.

I missed a lot of things and when I stepped outside I saw the end approaching fast.

I closed my eyes and I burnt away quickly.

I opened my eyes and I saw light; a tree ahead and a figure waiting for me. A familiar face, love, salvation, a new beginning in a place I thought didn't exist.

THE END?

I saw it on the news; *the world is about to end*, and I said to Sola, "Let's move into the tent," and she said, "We will still die if there's a war."

"Yeah, I know," I said. Of course I knew it, but I just thought it would be cooler to die in the tent as if we were explorers. So now we're inside the tent eating chocolate biscuits (our last meal?) and drinking hot cocoa, and I've got a whole bunch of graphic novels to go through before the end arrives.

These are the books that I've got:
Don Depresso, Volume 1 by Ruji Chaprik
Don Depresso, Volume 2 by Ruji Chaprik
Drinking at the Movies by Julia Wertz
Exit Wounds by Rutu Modan
Letting it Go by Miriam Katin

Right now I'm reading *A User's Guide to Neglectful Parenting* by Guy Delishe, and I'm going through the pages fast because I want to read all these novels before the end arrives. I should have read them ages ago but I always left it for the next day because I thought I had all the time in the world but I guess I was wrong and time itself is about to come to an end. Oh, to hell with it.

We're waiting for a bomb to fall, for something to happen, but there are rumours that this war is going to be silent and quick.

"How quick?" I wonder. "And will it be painless?"

And why war?

Why another war?

Who will win if we're all dead?

Doesn't anyone think about these things?

Sola also has a few books with her, poetry books of course, and they are:
Piano Rats by Franki Elliot
Half-Lit Houses by Tina Chang
Life on Mars by Tracy K. Smith

Right now she's pretending to read *Awe* by Dorothea Lasky, but I can tell she's scared and can't concentrate on the book she's reading. But who would want to read poetry at a time like this? Then again, when I called Julio he told me was reading Lorca for the first time. Bloody Lorca when the world is about to end?

But will it really end?

So far nothing has really happened and we haven't heard a thing on the news.

I put the book away and I tell Sola not to worry. "Let's finish the biscuits and the cocoa, and then let's light a joint. Maybe the idiots in power have changed their minds," I say.

"You think so?" she asks, hoping for the best, fearing the rest.

"Yeah, of course. They're always changing their minds when it comes to war," I say, but I too fear the worse.

We hug and we finish the biscuits and drink the cocoa, and then Sola says, "Something tastes funny."

And I feel it too, a strange taste in my mouth, something burning inside me slowly.

I say, "Let's kiss and see how our tongues taste."

She laughs and we kiss.

17-YEAR-OLD POET

A 17-year-old poet, armed with ignorance, and a bit of arrogance, too.

Still so naive, maybe still a virgin, he watches the world with concerned eyes.

He wants to write about love, and desire and masturbation, but, apart from desire and masturbation, what does he know about love?

And where is love?

Plenty of desire, that's true, desire for the things that can't satisfy the soul.

A burning desire for a materialistic world that concerns itself not with the human spirit but with what you've got.

And what do you have?

Love or an iPad?

The 17-year-old poet has dreams, and so much innocence, and he thinks that he can change the hearts of people with love, with words of love, written words of love, with poetry, but love itself is dying and the iGeneration want the iGadgets and to be someone else online.

As for the poet, he should concern himself with getting laid because the world will come to an end soon.

Sweating now, he gets his iPhone out and calls up a friend, a 19-year-old girl that fancies him, and when she answers the phone he asks if he can meet her, and when she says yes he runs down the steps, his heart beating fast, his cock hurting, and when he steps outside he notices that the streets are deserted.

He pedals to her house, only three miles away from his place, and he feels the end approaching, so he pedals fast, but the end is right on his trail, and he pedals even faster, but the end is right on his tail.

Minutes later, the bicycle lies abandoned on the street.

The poet's gone now.

His dreams have melted away, away with his love and the 19-year-old girl that was waiting for him.

2 - After the Apocalypse

THIS IS NOT THE END

"I love you." Those were the last words Nicole said to me just before I crashed. I was heading towards 5th Avenue, steering the wheel with one hand while holding the mobile phone with the other, and after she said those words, I looked up and I saw the yellow cab heading towards me. Last thing I remember seeing was me steering the wheel and then, bang, darkness. Total blackout.

I also remember hearing some noises; voices, sirens, screaming, but they were vague sounds which seem to come to me irregularly, and were then followed by long gaps of silence, until, finally, there was nothing but darkness and silence. But not even the darkness lasted forever because, after a while; minutes, seconds, days gone past; I don't know, I saw some light, a little light at the end of a corridor, or maybe it was a tunnel, and I walked towards the light, and as I walked I felt calm, but then I heard a voice saying, "Not yet," and not long after that I opened my eyes.

And now I'm here.

And I'm alone.

And there are tubes all over me.

I remove them one by one.

My body is bruised, parts of it have been bandaged, and my back hurts.

I'm wearing a hospital gown and nothing else underneath, and my head is bandaged.

After the tubes have been removed, I lie in bed for a few seconds more, just long enough to take a long, deep breath, and then I get up.

My feet touch the floor. The cold marble sends shivers running through my entire body. I look around and I see a pair of slippers next to a chair. Some clothes. They're my slippers. My clothes. Nicole must have brought them here but where is she now?

Where is my wife?

Where is my son?

Where is everyone?

(Where am I?)

I'm in a hospital, in a large room with four beds, three of them empty, and soon so will be mine. I get dressed slowly. Every movement is painful; a bone seems to snap, another bone hurts. I feel as if I've been in a boxing contest with Mike Tyson and Lennox Lewis, little me fighting against them both. I won, of course, but was badly beaten.

The beds have been left unmade, medicine and drinks have been left scattered on the floor, and as I make my way out of the hospital, I feel as if I'm a character in that British horror movie which was directed by Danny Boyle. Funnily enough I can remember the name of the movie's director but not its title. There's some kind of melted glue on the floor or some kind of liquid and I try not to step on it. Questions arise in my mind as I take little steps towards the front entrance: What's happening? Where's everyone? Will I see vampires or zombies or aliens when I step out of here?

Suddenly I feel the need to see someone, anyone, even a stranger, as long as he or she is friendly, and this is a bit ironic since I've always been a bit of a loner. But it is one thing to choose to be alone and another thing to have loneliness imposed on you.

Everything seems to have been switched off; no power, no lights, nothing beeping, nothing working. It looks as if the world has been disconnected. Once outside I see no major destruction apart from a few crashed cars. But where are the people? Where's everyone?

What made them leave their cars (and their houses) and where did they go?

I walk to the nearest house in front of me and I knock on the door. I knock and I kick. I repeat the process on three different houses and the response I get is always the same; nothing. No one.

I go inside two houses. I search through every room and nothing. Or should I say no one?

No power either.

This city that was once nerve-wrecking, filled with noise, alive 24 hours, is now a wall of silence.

I open a fridge and it stinks.

No cars driving by.

No birds singing.

No sirens.

No one.

Nothing.

Have I died?

Is this hell?

For years, while living the life of a novelist, I searched for solitude, and now I've got what I wanted.

Is this my own personal hell?

I leave this strange house and I step out onto the street, and I head towards a supermarket. There's glue everywhere, on the pavements, inside the cars, glue slowly melting away. So much glue. Where did it come from?

On the way to the supermarket I stop.

I'm not alone.

There's a man sitting down at *Starbucks*, a tramp. I've seen him before. For a moment I feel as if I'm dreaming and I approach the man slowly. He has seen me too, and he's staring at me too, but he doesn't look as shocked as I do. Next to him there's a pot of coffee and lots of canned food. My mouth gets watery as I stare at the food, and the tramp says, "Help yourself."

I open a can of corned beef, grab a plastic fork while the tramp fills up a cup of coffee for me, and then I take a bite. Hmm, no meal I've ever had tasted as good as this. Then I take a sip of coffee. Delicious too.

I keep on eating and drinking. Even though I've got a thousand questions to ask, for now they can all wait.

The tramp looks at ease as he drinks his coffee and reads *Burning Bright* by Ron Rash. He's now a king in this deserted city.

"What happened?" I finally ask, my mouth still filled with corned beef.

"Apocalypse," says the tramp.

"Apocalypse? Apocalypse when?" I ask.

"Two months ago."

"But what? Whom? Why?"

The tramp looks ahead, at the quietude around us, at a city where we seem to be the only habitants, but I'm sure there must be others out there, others like him, like me.

But where?

Where are they?

"There was a war, chemicals were released into the atmosphere, and whoever breathed those chemicals slowly melted away. The stuff got inside you and then slowly dissolved your body away," he says. "The quietest –and deadliest- war ever fought."

My brain reacts quickly and I ask, "The glue! The glue on the pavements and cars?"

"Life. Lives that were, lives that are gone."

"But what about you? Me?"

"I was underground, all the way underground, sleeping with the rats, and you were in a coma so you didn't breathe the chemicals."

"How do you know I was in a coma?"

"After the war was over, I still remained underground for a couple of weeks, and when I came up for fresh air, if you can call it that, I saw that there was no one left, no one that I could see, and I started to gather food, books and medicine. I went to the hospital where you were, searching for medicine, bandages and whatever I could use in case of sickness or an emergency, because you never know what can happen, especially now that we have no doctors, and I saw you in bed.

"At the time the electricity was still working so the machines were still working, but slowly, since there was no one left to look after the power, everything started to go off, including the machines that kept you going. Or maybe the ones in power switched if all off before going underground."

"Who started the war?"

"The usual suspects. Them. Us. Greedy people with no conscience about what they were doing."

Nothing of what he's saying makes sense (or maybe I don't want to believe him), and I still feel as if I'm stuck in a dream, with tubes coming out of me, a machine keeping me alive, turning life into fantasy.

"Did anyone win?" I ask.

"Does anyone wins in a war?" the tramp replies.

"Are there others out there?"

"Yes, I've seen a few, in another part of the city, but they've gone mad."

"Mad how?"

"You know, mad. Crazy."

"What do they do?"

"I don't know but last time I saw them they were smashing stuff."

"Stuff?"

"Yes, stuff. Cars. Windows. Cars windows. Furniture. Even walls. Stuff."

"Why?"

"Because they are crazy."

"How did they survive?"

"How the hell should I know? Maybe they were hiding underground."

"What about the government? Did anyone survive? You mention them going underground. Shouldn't someone be doing something about this?"

"You ask too many questions. I understand; you're scared but there's no need for it. Not for now. Anyway, more coffee?"

I nod yes and he refills my cup. And then we enjoy the silence for a few minutes more.

The tramp rolls a cigarette and then I ask if I can have one too and he hands me the tobacco and papers. We're living through the apocalypse and it's so relaxing. Who would have thought that?

The area where we are has been neatly organised by the tramp. He has bottled water in one side of the room, right next to hundreds of cans of food, lots of books, too, and to prepare coffee, he boils the water in a pan on a fire, and then, *presto*, the black delicious liquor is ready.

"What will happen when you run out of food?" I ask.

"I'll move on, or I'll stay here and gather more food. Who knows? What's the point of making so many plans and worry too much about life?"

I say nothing. Maybe he's right (about what?), maybe he's wrong. The world is dead, or almost dead, so what's the point of worrying too much now?

Above us the sky is red, the clouds are brown, the water that runs through the tap is black, just like the hearts of the people that started the apocalypse.

"I live nearby," I say. My voice sounds strange, a bit teary, weak, almost unfamiliar to me. I cough. Once. Twice. Phlegm comes out of my mouth. I spit it out. I drink more coffee. Black and bitter, just like the world that has been left behind for the survivors. I eat canned fruit, its juice so delicious.

The world is dying and I'm having a picnic.

Flashbacks of my life start to haunt me.

"I live nearby," I say it again as I try to get my voice back, gather some strength, but I can't deny it; I'm scared, scared of what will be.

My grandparents managed to evade the Nazis, my parents died young, and now I'm facing the apocalypse. Can't a poor Jew have a break?

"What's your name?" I ask.

"Yu Hua," the tramp replies.

"Yu Hua? Like the Chinese author?" But the tramp isn't Chinese.

"Yes. I am he."

"But you're not Chinese."

"Says whom?"

"I do."

"And who are you? What's your name?"

"I'm Elias Piëch."

"The novelist? Good. I see you're learning quickly. After the apocalypse you can be whoever you want."

"But I am Elias Piëch!"

"And I'm Yu Hua."

"But you're not Chinese!"

"Says who?"

"I do!"

"And who are you?"

"Oh G-d."

"I don't think He exists."

"Who?"

"G-d. Where is He? Why did He let the apocalypse happen?"

I shrug my shoulders. Maybe He let it happen so that we could learn from our mistakes and start again. This is what I think but I keep it for myself.

The sun shows no sign of leaving the sky. Bored, I ask, "How long before it gets dark?"

"The days are longer now."

"What about the White House? Anyone in there?"

"Not that I know. The last time I heard the news, the president and his people were heading to Denver Airport International. Now there's no news."

I stare at the red sun and the brown clouds. What an ugly world our leaders have left behind.

I miss the moon. I miss the night.

I miss my family.

92

I miss sounds around me. The sounds of life. The noisy engines on the street. Aeroplanes in the sky. Birds singing. Dogs barking.

Sidewalks that were once flooded with people are now empty, the remains of humanity slowly melting away. Chaos and noise have been replaced by an eerie silence. The city is now an empty jungle.

What now?

"What now?" I ask.

The trump shrugs his shoulders.

"We keep on living," he says.

He's right.

I get up from my seat and I thank him for everything, but it is time for me to go and check out my home.

"No problem," he says.

"Will you be here later?"

"Probably."

"What about tomorrow?"

"Maybe."

His answer is the right one. Nothing is certain now so instead of saying yes or no, he says probably or maybe.

I leave the café and start retracing the steps that will take me home. The first steps have been taken and I'm already dreading what I won't find there.

Every building is still intact, as is every tree, every single machine, even though many of them –the machines- don't work anymore, and with the passage of time the grass will start growing, taking over the concrete.

I turn around to take one last look at the tramp and he remains sitting, smoking without a care in the world. And what else can he do now but enjoy these moments of peace?

As I make my way home I try to imagine what kind of devious minds could have conceived a weapon that managed to wipe out most of the humanity without blowing a single brick away. Too bad that those minds didn't use their knowledge for something more worthwhile.

Maybe I should have asked the tramp more about these crazies that have survived (Are they friendly? Are they armed?), but I'm confused, still trying to take all of this in, and I feel weak, afraid of what's happening, afraid of the world, because even though most of humanity are dead, some still remain, and sooner or later gangs will be formed and bad people will become even worse, and more death will follow.

Halfway home I stop by a shoe shop. I still have my slippers on but I need something better than this. How come Nicole didn't bring me a better pair of shoes while I was at the hospital? Maybe she was going to before the apocalypse happened. And maybe she's there, at the hospital, alongside our son, their bodies now gone, turned to nothing.

I put on a pair of socks and a comfortable pair of running shoes. I leave the sport shop and I cross the road. The sun is slowly slipping away as night approaches. I can't wait to see the moon.

I walk into a supermarket and I fill up a trolley with canned food, bottled water, medicine and candles. Good thing I live on the ground flood. I pick up a book that someone left behind at the counter; *A Minor Apocalypse* by Tadeusz Konwicki. *A Minor Apocalypse*? Even now Life still knows how to throw in a joke or two.

I push the trolley all the way home, and as I'm approaching my building I see Nicole's bike locked outside, and my mind travels back in time, and I see us, as a family; Nicole and me and our son Abraham, and I leave the trolley behind and run home, and as I run I also leave tears behind.

I shout out their names, "Nicole! Abraham! Nicole! Abraham!" but, as I feared, there's no reply, and no one comes to their windows to look at me. I am alone (and I am not legend).

I reach the door but it is locked. Did the locked door manage to keep the apocalypse away? I bang on it and I hear the rattling in my pockets. Keys. I reach for them. I enter the building.

Silence.

A dreadful silence.

After the apocalypse will there be a new Septet by a new Beethoven? What about a Mona Lisa by a da Vinci or a Statue of David by Michelangelo? Who will teach the survivors how to play instruments? Will four boys from Liverpool form a band and call themselves The Snails? Will a new Boss be born in the USA?

Pictures, the pictures of those I love keep me company while I stare at a red moon. Why is the sky so red?

A dreary silence coming from outside shows me that this is not a dream. It is a nightmare.

I look at the pile of records in front of me; Gershwin, Debussy, Chopin, Duran Duran, Chic…I can't listen to any of them.

Will a new Proust emerge from the ashes and say, "Okay, I'll be the first narrator of the after-apocalypse. I can even use some of the words that Proust used and no one will be able to tell the difference."

But how will books be published?

And who will read them?

After shedding a river of tears, to pass the time I do what I always do; I read and I write; I write little entries in a notepad. A few poems, too. The loneliness grows but time seems to stand still.

And how will the new Beatles record their music?

History has taught me that no matter what happens only one thing is certain; there will always be a new evil around the corner, a new dictator, a preacher of evil, a being blinded by power and guided by corruption and greed.

The writing and reading wears me out, and pretty soon I find my mind drifting away with my thoughts all over the place, and I want to cry a bit more, a lot more, but I can't cry; there are no more tears left in me, so I just lie in bed, the curtains open, the windows closed, and I stare at the moon until I fall asleep.

Midwives.
After the apocalypse we will need midwives.
Nurses.
Doctors.
Poets.
But will they want to be something else?
What if there's a fire?
Who will put the fire out?
Won't we need fire-fighters?
And police to deal with gangs?
In every futuristic movie there are always gangs.

Okay, maybe not in every futuristic movie: I'm thinking about the *Mad Max* movies, and that Patrick Swayze movie, *Steel Dawn*.

The Postman with Kevin Costner.

Waterworld, too.

Is Kevin still alive?

And movies?

Who will make movies now that we don't have the technology?

All the bands will be acoustic; Tracy Chapman and Suzanne Vega will make a comeback, and we'll be stuck with theatre.

I'll write stories in notepads and then I'll read them out loud. But to whom?

Who will listen to my stories?

In the morning, when I open my eyes, I lie in bed for a few minutes more, and I wait for something, for a noise, for a familiar face to walk in through the door, but there's no one, there is nothing, nothing but silence.

After I get changed I eat a can of tuna, followed by another can of tuna, and I drink a warm can of Coke. The red sun is out with a few brown clouds covering the sky. I roll a cigarette and I stand by the window watching the passiveness of the city.

No cars driving by.

No birds.

No people.

Damn it, this is definitely a nightmare.

I wonder if my wife and son have survived, and if they have, where are they? And if they're okay I hope they have survived, but if they aren't okay, I'd rather they be dead because it is better to be dead than to be in pain, extreme pain, dying bit by bit, dying slowly.

I miss bread. Plain bread and butter. Warm bread, straight out of the oven, and then the butter melting slowly on top of the bread.

Freshly ground coffee.

Cubes of ice.

Watermelon.

I miss a lot of things but what I miss the most are the faces of my wife and my son and the sound of life.

I miss you.
Who are you?
Where are you?

I leave the building and I go out to meet the tramp. I wonder if he's at *Starbucks* today. The world comes to an end and the survivors still meet at *Starbucks*.

I never read Lee Rourke or Andrew Miller. Or Ben Brooks. But that's okay.

There's a bicycle leaning on a lamppost outside the building, a bicycle which I'm sure wasn't here yesterday. There's a note too, blue-tacked to the bicycle.

Come to my place for coffee.
Yu Hua
☺

It's always good to know that there is someone out there waiting for you, a familiar face. It's always good to know that you aren't alone.

The road is all mine but I miss the traffic, the harsh looks on the faces of some of the drivers, and I miss the smiles on the children's faces as I pedalled past them. Every building, every house looks empty, but the tramp (I can't get used to call him Yu Hua) told me there are others out there.
Note to myself: Ask Yu Hua –I mean the tramp- more about the others.

The tramp's sitting on the same spot as yesterday, still wearing the same clothes, and that makes me think; why hasn't he changed clothes yet? He's a king now in this empty area, a king without a crown but with plenty of coffee available. This morning I notice that he has plenty of clean clothes hanging on a chair, but why isn't he wearing them?

"I'm waiting for the rain," he says, and he looks up, to the sky, and my eyes follow his, and I notice that the clouds are changing colour.

The tramp has left big empty bins outside to collect water from the rain and some of that water he will then use to wash himself and the rest he will boil and use it to make coffee or whatever. The tramp, now a king named Yu Hua, is slowly building his own kingdom.

We drink coffee, smoke rolled tobacco, and eat bags of crisps. I ask him about the crazies.

"I don't know who they are. I saw them breaking stuff and I hid. Whenever you see someone breaking stuff without a reason, you should always hide," says Yu Hua.

"Where are they?" I ask.

"I won't tell you because if I do you'll be curious and you will go and see them. Stay hidden. Stay where you are."

"But they could come here at any time."

"Nah. Not yet, anyway. They're crazy and lazy and I think they are building some sort of fort, and, for now at least, they're sticking to their own area."

"What about you? What are you going to do?"

"I'll remain here for a bit longer, until I get bored, but I think that I would like to see the world."

"But how will you travel? You can't cycle everywhere."

"Yeah, that's true. I guess I'll just see my country. Later, who knows? Maybe I'll get a boat."

I stay with him for a couple of hours and all we do is smoke and talk. When I'm about to leave Yu Hua tells me about a shop near my place where I can get a typewriter, ribbons and some paper.

"You should keep a diary. Your book could be the first after-the-apocalypse book," he says.

That's a good idea. I even get a bit upset for not having thought of that. But who will read it?

I thanked him once more for everything and waved him goodbye, and he told me to get ready for the rain and have a shower because I smelled, and so did he, and then I cycled to the shop that Yu Hua had told me about and there was a nice, red Olivetti waiting there for me. I searched around for a shoulder bag, grabbed the biggest one, put the typewriter inside it, some ribbons, too, and paper, and then I grabbed a couple of bottles of wine and some cigars from another shop, and afterwards I pedalled home. And when I got home I spent a few hours in front of the typewriter writing about the last two days. I wrote down some thoughts, too. While I was writing I felt so alive. Later on I cried and I felt dead inside. And then I wrote a bit more to stay alive.

Yu Hua was right. It rained last night and it is still raining this morning. When the rain started to fall down I got undressed and I went outside for a shower. Then I walked naked along the city, got some clean bins from a shop nearby, and now they're filled with water, still standing outside, waiting for me to bring them inside.

But this morning I'm tired, just a bit tired, and I don't think I'll go anywhere.

For breakfast I have pickles, pickled eggs, and anchovies with some crackers. I also manage to boil some water and I drink instant coffee. For lunch I have the rest of the pickles, pickled eggs, anchovies, and crackers, and I drink a bottle of wine, and afterwards, feeling a bit drunk, a bit dizzy, so sad for being alone, I lie on the sofa for a long time.

The shelves are covered in dust, and the records and books too, but I can't be bothered to clean a thing. Not now. Not yet. Maybe never.

An orchestra.
A choir.
A couple of violins. There are two in the living room, one belonging to Nicole and one to Abraham, both unused now, gathering dust.
A piano.
Bach.
Lou Gramm.
Bill Bryson.
Pamela Anderson.
Barbra Streisand.
Jerry.
Seinfeld.
Jerry.
Springer.

Jerry.
Lee Lewis.
Jerry.
And Tom.

I doze off and names and faces and things pop in and out of my dreams, my mind, my memories, memories of things past, remembrance of things past, time, Proust, Proust and time.
And madeleines.

Dinner time, I step out and I cross the road. I go to the old Asian shop where I get dried fruit, some *chilli con carne*, canned of course, crackers, olives, and then I go next door, to the Italian restaurant which has a fine selection of wines, and I sit at a table on my own.
The city is engulfed in darkness and silence.
Not a light on sight.
Not a single light.
I light a cigar and I open a bottle of wine.
I make no plans for tomorrow.
What would be the point of it?

Pizza…

A cappuccino…

Next morning, late in the day and I'm still in bed, not sleeping, just staring at the ceiling, when I hear someone knocking on my front door. Scared, I make my way out of bed slowly. The front door is unlocked so whoever is outside could just enter the room. As I make my way along the living room I know straight away who is knocking. I open the front door and Yu Hua is standing there with a smile on his face. He brought some coffee. He looks different. He's wearing a clean track suit, new trainers, and he has trimmed his beard.
We drink coffee and we eat crackers.
"If only we had some cheese," says Yu Hua, and his words seem to fly right through me, and then I take a ride with those words and we fly through the atmosphere, looking for cheese, for butter, bread, and other people, too.

"Come on, let's get some exercise," he says. "How do you feel about going to the Yankees Stadium to hit a few balls?"

"Sounds good," I say boringly.

Mother Nature is slowly taking over the city. Grass stretches itself out of the concrete, slowly but surely, with little green bits starting to find a way out of that concrete jungle, and, dear G-d, I'm sure I've just seen a bee.

I stop and Yu Hua asks me what's wrong.

I raise a finger and I point at the sky. We're not alone anymore. The city has another habitant, one who buzzes past us.

"A bee!" he says.

"A bee," I say.

"How did it get here?" he asks.

"I don't know but I guess it's a good sign."

What about honey?

If all the bees die will we have to make fake honey?

What about love?

Why is it so hard for us to love one another?

Imagine that the world ends and only a few of us are left standing?

What religion will we choose?

What if we choose none?

What if we choose not to believe?

Can we still get along?

But look at how many religions we had and look what we did even though we were all supposed to believe in something?

Look at the mess we're in, and we believed in something, we all shouted that our religion was the right one, and then we killed and killed and killed, in the name of...

Stupidity?

"Ah, beautiful. I always dreamed of playing here," says Yu Hua as he stands in a corner of the Yankees Stadium staring at the empty seats, at the empty stadium. Emptiness everywhere we look.

Again, my eyes might be deceiving me (but I did see the bee so they weren't deceiving me the first time), but I think that the sky is becoming cleaner, gaining the colour of the past. True, the clouds are still a bit brownish but not as brown as yesterday, and the sun is a dirty-ash-brown, but not as brown as yesterday.

We have put on our baseball uniforms and I carry two bags loaded with balls while Yu Hua carries the bat in his right hand with a big smile on his face. The grass needs cutting, a good trim, that's for sure, but we're not worried about it.

Yu Hua lays down the rules.

"You throw and I hit," he says.

"Okay. I'll give it a go," I say.

I don't know how many balls he hits but I know that he misses more than he hits, and by the end of it my right arm is really sore.

On the way back to our respective homes I ask Yu Hua if he will take me to where he saw the crazies but he says no.

"I don't want to go there," he says and I don't discuss the matter any further.

But later at night, while I lie in bed, my right arm sore as hell, I decide that, come next morning, I'll go a bit further on my travels. If others have survived there's a chance that my wife and son could be alive too, and that little hope is all I need to keep me going. If there's no hope what's the point of living?

It is lashing outside on the next morning, torrential rain that never seems to stop, and as the minutes go by the drops turn to hail, and so I stay indoors. My arm is aching so I take a few painkillers, and in the morning I lie on the sofa and I read a book by Chloe Aridjis. For breakfast, I eat three cans of fruit, all washed down with coffee, and I smoke a couple of cigarettes while sitting by the window; curtains open but the windows closed.

Alone with my thoughts, as I stare at the emptiness outside, the rain falling down from the sky, clearing the mess that Man has left behind, I can't help but think about my family, and even the image of the tramp comes to my mind. Loneliness, when imposed on us by the circumstances, is a terrible thing to endure.

In the afternoon, after I have a little nap and a few more painkillers, my arm isn't as sore as it was in the morning, and to pass the time, instead of reading, I write. I put my old laptop away, a machine that is of no use now, and then I carry the typewriter to the desk. But before I start writing I go downstairs and make sure that the front door of the building is locked. I've been a bit careless for the last two days, but if the tramp is right and there are a few crazies out there, one can never be too careful.

I write everything that comes to my mind, every little thought, and while I'm writing I think, "Wouldn't it be wonderful if I could listen to a bit of Bach?"

The things we take for granted, like music and love, and even bread and clean water, are the things we miss the most once they are gone.

When it gets darker I make the usual walk across the road, first to the supermarket and then to the Italian restaurant, and I eat canned food and drink a bottle of wine, and afterwards I smoke a cigar, and I look like a king in an isolated kingdom, a king without a crown, worst of all, a king without a queen.

Next morning, another dateless and nameless day, I write a bit more, about the past and the present; what's the point of writing about the future? Will there even be one? And afterwards, bored of doing the same thing day in, day out, I grab a shoulder bag, a couple of bottles of water (no need for food because I can stop anywhere and grab a bite to eat; then again, I can also grab something to drink - but I take the water with me), a notebook and a pen just in case I want to write some notes down, and I get on my bicycle and go for a ride along the city.

The rain has stayed away for the day, at least for now, but the air is cold, which is fine by me because I'd rather pedal in the cold than under the scorching heat. For a moment, as I pedal nowhere (and everywhere), I feel I've gone back in time as I pedal past the places of the past, cafés and bars and shops which I've been to various times, but, unlike the past, those places are now empty, looking like a mirage in a desert populated with dead machines.

I also feel ageless, which is a bit silly, but that's how I feel because there are no clocks to tell the time, and no one knows what day it is, meaning time has stopped and there are no birthdays to attend or even to pass on my own.

When I get tired I stop by a shop and I eat whatever is available. I bring the bicycle inside the shop. Just in case. Sometimes it is good to be a bit paranoid because paranoia, or extreme precaution, can save us from nasty surprises.

I eat crackers with tuna, crackers with anchovies, and I even find some pickled eggs in a jar. I take a bite of one. It tastes good, nothing to fear, and I end up eating three eggs. I drink a can of soda, and afterwards, still feeling a bit hungry, and thirsty, too, I eat a bag of crisps and drink a bottle of water. And it is while I'm still inside the shop that I hear noises, while I'm still masticating the crisps, and they are loud noises, screams; not of pain but of anger. I put the bottle of water down and, carefully and silently, I step out of the shop. I push the bicycle alongside me instead of riding it because I don't want to be seen and I must walk carefully.

In every movie that I've watched, or books that I've read, after the apocalypse there are always a few nasty characters left behind, and the lonely hero must battle against the odds to survive.

But I'm no hero.

I'm just a tired Jew lost in the ghetto.

I follow the noises and after a while they die down. Still, I tread carefully, in search of life; a familiar face, too, please, a friendly face, please.

The road gets tighter, not to mention messier, with abandoned cars taking over the whole place. But were these cars abandoned or were the drivers behind the wheel or on the passengers' seats when the apocalypse arrived? I guess I'll never know. Right now that's not even important and I guess I can write the apocalypse however I feel like it. Historians to come, if there are any, will then take my word for it so I can write whatever I want; even make myself look like the hero of the after-apocalypse.

But what is a hero?

Is a hero someone who saves someone else or someone who tries his best to survive against all odds?

Or both (and a lot more)?

I know that I'm on the right track when I see smashed plates, broken bottles, battered cars, and broken doors around me. Destruction and chaos is the path chosen by the weaker minds in times of trouble, and as I follow the trail of madness, I know that I should turn around and get out of there, but if I do that what kind of witness will I be to the end of times? More importantly, what will I write about if I see nothing?

I move forward, and when the pile of destruction gets bigger, I have to leave my bicycle behind and climb over cars and garbage.

Ahead of me chairs lie abandoned, all of them looking as if they have been used not so long ago. Or maybe not. Maybe I'm just saying they've been used not so long ago to make the story more interesting. But they do look like they've been used because they're facing a wall, a wall where someone has drawn a large black swastika. And a swastika is always bad news for a Jewish person. And I'm Jewish and I shouldn't be here. And I'm not alone.

Three men with unfriendly faces are making their way towards me. Two of them are armed with swords while the other one is holding a baseball bat. I've got nothing with me. No weapon. No malice. Definitely no chance either.

I start moving backwards slowly while they march silently towards me. Soon enough their pace becomes hurried and I start running with them giving me chase.

After the apocalypse no one says a lot.
What's there left to say?
What about languages?
What languages will we learn?
Who will want to learn Hebrew?
Japanese?
Lhasa Tibetan?

I run fast through the pile of cars and destruction but my pursuers run faster than I, and to make matters worse I slip and I fall, and I land on a puddle. I look up and I see a sword coming towards me but then the arm carrying the sword falls next to me and the crazy is screaming. A tall, bald man, dressed entirely in black, seems to materialize out of nowhere, and he too is holding a samurai sword. And in the next few seconds he kills the crazies and sends them back to hell.

The tall man looks just like Steven Seagal, but he's bald and has a long beard, and Steven Seagal isn't bald and he doesn't has a long beard. Speechless and scared, I look at him and then at the three dead crazies lying on the ground next to me. I get up slowly, my eyes fixed on the dead bodies and on the stranger. He looks at me and says, "You better get out of here quickly."

"Who are you?" I ask.

"I'm Steven Seagal," he says.

After the apocalypse, if you've survived, you can be whoever you want. Rename yourself and start a new life. Most of all, be good.

"Steven Seagal isn't bald and he doesn't has a beard that long," I say.

"I shaved my head and I grew a beard. Anyway, I was getting bald so what the hell? What about you? What's your name?"

"I'm Elias Piëch."

"Are you being funny? I've just saved your ass and that's how you thank me?"

"No. Really. I'm Elias Piëch, the novelist."

"But I heard that Elias died in a car crash."

"I didn't die. I was in a coma."

"Really?"

"Really. Honest to G-d."

"No blasphemy, young man. Whoever you are, you better get the hell out of here because he's coming."

"Who's coming?"

"The main bad guy."

"Can't you defeat him?"

"I'm afraid not."

"But you're Steven Seagal."

"Hmm. I think I'm going to change my name soon. I'm getting too old for this action-hero stuff."

"Where are you going?"

"Underground."

Steven, or whoever this stranger is, lifts a drain cover and retreats underground. His head still popping out of the hole, I ask, "Can I go with you?"

"Sorry, buddy. I travel alone. You better go now," he says, and then he puts the lid over the drain. I think about following him but I'm scared of how he would react to it.

Up ahead, standing on top of a pile of cars, there's a strange creature, something that looks like a cross between animal and human, or some kind of mutant. A deformity of the apocalypse or the carrier of evil. Or both. The creature is staring at me and then it raises its right hand in the air, and, pointing a finger at me, it says, "KILL THE JEW!"

And I hear the screams coming from behind the creature, and I hear the footsteps, too, and I run even before I get to see the faces.

I run to where my bicycle is and I hear the screams coming from behind me, but I dare not to look at the faces. Not yet.

I get on the bicycle and I pedal out of there as fast as I can. At first I don't even bother to look back, but once I've got a good rhythm going I take a look behind me and I see a few men and women giving me chase. No signs of the creature though, and that's good news.

The crazies chase me for a long time, almost all the way to the bridge, but they tire soon enough and they stop, their mouths gasping for air, and I stop too, a good distance separating us now, and I take one good look at their faces; faces filled with hate and fatigue.

For the next few seconds, I stare at them, expecting to see the creature one more time, but then, after giving it some good thought, I decide it's better not to stay there tempting faith so I cycle the hell out of there.

Yu Hua is no longer at *Starbucks*. His bicycle is gone too and he left a note for me.

> *I've moved on.*
> *You better move soon too before they arrive.*
> *Yu Hua*
> ☹

I go back to my place for the last time. I grab the typewriter and my notes and I put them in a bag alongside pictures of my wife and son. Then I'm out of there too.

Day becomes night so quickly without me even noticing it. Alone in a strange house, hiding from the crazies and the creature, I flick the ash into the air carelessly, knowing that I won't have to clean the mess I leave behind, and I face the wall in front of me where framed pictures of strangers stare at me, pictures of a happy family, and I can't help but search in my bag for the pictures of my family.

Before I go to sleep I make sure that every door is blocked so that no one can enter the house without me hearing it. I also plan a quick escape route by getting a rope ready for me to climb down the wall on the back of the house. Of course, if the crazies happen to be waiting for me by my escape route I'm screwed. But no plan is ever perfect and one can only hope for the best.

I pray, in the morning, in the afternoon, at night, but who is listening to my prayers?

In the morning I'm up earlier than usual, and after scanning the area outside with a pair of binoculars that I got from a shop, I leave the house and I keep on cycling with no clear destination on my mind. But I cycle slowly; I go easy on me. The face of the deformed creature that I saw yesterday is still so clear in my mind. What was that?

It only had one eye, right in the middle of its face, its flesh was reddish, and although the rest of its features looked human, it certain wasn't a human being. But what kind of creature was it? And the words it said: "Kill the Jew!" How does it know that I'm Jewish?

Thinking about the creature makes me pedal a bit faster.

I'm now in Geneseo, a town just outside Rochester, eating a meal by the Bear Fountain. As far as I can tell the town is empty. I almost moved into the historic Big Tree Inn but I've decided to rest in a little home instead of a big hotel.

I travelled for days, maybe weeks, maybe longer, and during that time I didn't saw a living soul but I'm sure I saw a rabbit in Syracuse. I've swapped bicycles twice and my latest is a Trek Soho, and I carry my typewriter and notes in a bike trailer. I've got some food in there, too, plus water. A couple of books too; *Asunder* by Chloe Aridjis and *Sputnik Sweetheart* by Haruki Murakami. I've found them in someone's house, two books and nothing else. Did the habitants of that house escaped, I wonder?

I've been so busy going from place to place, and writing down some notes, that I didn't had time to read a page of either of those books, but tonight, and maybe tomorrow too, I will rest and read, and make some plans, too. Yes, plan ahead, plan for the future, for however short-lived that future might be. A person should have some goals, for as little as they may be, because if we don't, we will be living on empty. Life hasn't ended. It has simply changed and I need to keep on living and believing. My family is gone, probably "erased" out of this planet, but I've been left behind for a reason, or so I would like to think, and I still say the *Sh'ma*, and other prayers, too, and, if anything, my faith is stronger than before, and I know that I must keep on living a righteous life, a better life than the one I used to live.

In the past I was a bit selfish and now I must change.

I remain in Geneseo for three nights and I get some work done on my journal. After being on the road for so long, my body needs the rest, and I spend most of the time indoors, reading and writing and resting. On the fourth morning I leave Geneseo and I head towards Hamburg, a town in Erie County, just by the sea, a place I know so well and where I spent some good moments in the past.

My left knee is giving me problems. At times the bones feel as if they're trapped or tied together, and when I stretch my left leg I feel the bones snap.

There are so many abandoned cars around me, a lot of them with the keys still on, but I'd rather pedal than to drive a car. A car makes noise, therefore attracts a lot of attention. Even now, when my left knee feels like it's going to quit on me, I still pedal forward.

Coming to Hamburg was a mistake. A big mistake. Most of the town is ashes, burned to the ground. I wonder what happened to it. Did someone left something in the oven before the apocalypse started?

I haven't written a thing in seven days. I mark the days on a wall. There's not a lot happening so there isn't a lot to write about. But one thing happened yesterday which I must write about. I saw a fish. I saw a fish in the river, moving slowly along the water. And this morning I saw more fish. And fruit is also starting to grow on trees. Fruit and fish. I feel as if I'm in Paradise. Maybe coming here wasn't a mistake after all.

I've been here now for the last 434 days, meaning I've been here, in Hamburg, for more than a year. I've started to grow vegetables in a little back garden in the home where I live, and every once in a while I go fishing, and I always manage to catch something. Little by little life is improving.

I read every single Paul Auster, Roberto Bolaño and Thomas Bernhard book at the library. I've started to read Musil but couldn't get into it. I quit halfway through *Ulysses* too, and I've started to read Proust.

1055 days, I think, or maybe I just make marks on the wall without even knowing it. Damn it, I'm going a bit crazy.

I honestly don't know how long I've been here. Ten years maybe? More? Less? I've stopped making marks on the wall long time ago.

Some days I sing because I miss the sound of music. Hey, the sound of music. That reminds me of Julie Andrews and Falco.
And Amadeus.

Yesterday, while browsing through an old house, I found books by Najat El Hachmi, Wang Shuo, and Josip Novakovich, writers whose works I hadn't yet read. The books were in bad conditions, the pages yellowish and brownish but still readable, so I took them home. I found a can of beef, expire date on it 2017, and when I opened it the meat still looked okay. I took a bite and it tasted good so I took it home too, along with the books, and then I fried it. The meat, not the books.

I'm feeling old.
Tired.
Depressed.

So much happened yesterday and I must write about it. This diary had been forgotten but now the plot is thickening and I must write in it.
A woman!
I saw a woman in the forest.
Or should I say a young girl?
She looked to be around seventeen-years-old and she was swimming in a lake, her skin as white as snow. I saw a man too and I killed him. But wait, I'm jumping ahead; I'm revealing too much and

not saying a lot. This is what happened: I left home early in the morning, and I went out for a long ride. Lucky for me, I decided to take the typewriter and the notes with me. I wanted to go through them and write a bit, write about the changes around me. With the passage of time, as Mother Nature takes over the concrete, everything around me has changed so much and I wanted to see it all, witness the beginning of a New World. Where once ago there had been no trees, there was now a large forest with trees growing slowly, coming out of the ground as if by magic.

And birds, too!

Yes, two birds.

Two birds standing on a tree, scanning the area as if they were Mother Nature's guardians, the two main witnesses of the New World. What about me? Wasn't I a witness too? Later on those two birds would become the witnesses to my crime.

I cycled along the river for as long as I could, and then I stopped by a big tree, hid my bicycle and belongings in the woods, and after a snack I kept on walking.

My eyes were admiring Mother Nature's beauty, but, tired of being on my own, I missed the city lights, the noise and chaos, the days of yesteryear, years gone by and which I probably would never see the likes of it anymore, and as I made my way along the forest I thought I heard noises. Splashing noises. I stopped for a moment and I listened carefully. I thought I was going slightly crazy but then I heard it again, the splashing, and I moved a bit faster.

I cut through the forest looking like a madman, a soul possessed, a soul on the brink of insanity, a man who could no longer separate illusion from reality, and I was moving so fast I looked like a marathon runner that had been on a diet of dope. But no; it wasn't dope that drove me forwards. It was hope. Hope of seeing another human being. And just then, years gone past since I last saw him, the face of Yu Hua returned to my mind. I wondered what had happened to the tramp. Where was he now? Was he still alive? What about the crazies and the one-eye-creature?

And just as I was thinking about them I saw her; a woman, her naked body splashing against the water, her skin so white and pure, like milk.

Tears came to my eyes as I stood there staring at her.

A woman.

The first woman of flesh and blood that I had seen in years.

I'm ashamed to admit it but I did have a few books with photos of naked women lying around at my place, but the photos were nothing when compared to the real thing.

I stood there, transfixed, hypnotized, staring at her for a few good minutes, admiring her naked flesh. A few minutes went by before she finally saw me, and when she did, she too froze and stared at me. I lifted my hand slowly in the air, as if I was a child, but she didn't react to my greeting. She started to make her way out of the water slowly, her eyes fixed on mine, and as I diverted my eyes from her briefly I saw a pile of clothes on top of a rock. Her clothes. That's where she was heading to.

Fearing that I might lose her once she got dressed, I run towards her along the sea, while she too started to run while still in the water. Needless to say, I got to her before she got dressed, and when I grabbed her arm she tried to wrestle me, but even though I'm not what you can call a strong man, I managed to pin her down to the ground, and as my knees lay on top of her arms, I said, "I mean you no harm."

She said nothing. She just laid there; eyes wide open, looking scared.

"I mean you no harm," I said it again, but the truth was I was no longer capable of controlling my emotions. My hands, my eyes, my whole body was in turmoil, dying to touch her, to have her, make her mine and only mine. I reached for her breasts and I caressed them slowly, gently, while the young girl kept staring at me, looking even more frightened. Evil thoughts started to run through my mind, but then I remembered who I was, what I had learned, and I realised if she was here there must be others, and then I wondered if she was one of the crazies. I put my hands up quickly and I said, "I'm sorry. I'm so sorry."

I started to get up when a blow from behind sent me down to the ground. A warm liquid run down my neck. By instinct, I touched it and I saw that it was blood. My blood. My head was pounding and my legs felt like jelly when I tried to stand up. Still on the ground, I looked around and I saw the young woman getting dressed. And then I saw a bearded man heading towards me. With his long white beard, for a moment he reminded me of my good friend Rabbi Teller. But the man in front of me wasn't a Rabbi. Worst of all, he was armed and he didn't look as if he were a friend. The young woman quickly got dressed and then ran out of there. As for me, I tried to reason with my aggressor.

"I'm so sorry. I didn't mean to touch her. I'm so sorry. It has been a long time since I last saw a woman, or another human being for that matter, and..." I said but he cut me off.

"Save your breath," my aggressor said. "Words can't save you now."

"I'm Elias Piëch, the novelist," I said, hoping the stranger would know who I was.

"Really? Isn't that sweet? My brother John was a novelist too," he said.

I was up, facing him, trying not to stare at the knife, trying to reason with him, but he started to advance towards me, the knife up in the air, aimed at me.

"Before I kill you, I want to thank you. You see, now I can rape the girl, and kill her afterwards, and then I will blame it all on you. And I'll tell you a secret, too. I'm the BogMan," he said, and then he launched forward, the knife missing my right arm by an inch because, in that same instant, moved by the sheer will of surviving, I moved to the left, and then I punched him on his neck with all my strength and he fell down. And he stayed down and didn't move.

I kicked him softly a couple of times, and then I kneeled down and turned him over. He was dead. When I punched him on the neck he fell down on his own knife and, therefore, killed himself. Isn't karma a bitch? Or something?

Filled with terror and panic, I run out of there as quickly as I could without bothering to look for the young woman, and once I reached my bicycle, I pedalled out of there without even looking back. But the day and the surprises weren't yet over as there were a few more nasty surprises waiting for me around the corner.

As I pedalled home I heard familiar noises coming from nearby. I stopped, still in shock, and I listened carefully. Those loud noises: what were they?

So familiar yet I couldn't recall what they were.

But then it hit me!

Car engines!

I pedalled slowly, my emotions on the edge. Unsure of what was happening I let my bicycle hidden in the woods, and then I sneaked back to town on foot.

I saw the crazies in what was then my house, going through my garden and belongings. One of them came running out of the house, holding on his hands a copy of the *Tanakh*, and then he screamed at the top of his lungs: "JEW!"

The crazies went even crazier, as if that was possible (but it was and I saw it), and then I saw it again; the creature, the one-eye-creature, the beast, a being the likes I've never seen before, now a bit aged too, like all of us.

The creature said, "Burn the book, find the Jew, and kill him."

The creature was the anti-Semite, the hater of all that is righteous and good, the one who fears love itself.

My little paradise destroyed by the crazies, I made my way back to where I left my bicycle and, fortunately, my diary too, but not a lot of food, and then I left town.

Later I cried because I had lost everything, including the pictures of my family, and I would have to start all over again. And the pictures could never be replaced.

I cycled for a long time. When night came I ignored the darkness and kept on pedalling.

I felt sad because there were other human beings out there (and the creature) but they had gone crazy and I would probably remain on my own for the rest of my life. That is if they don't catch me first and kill me.

And now I need to stop writing and rest for a bit. I'm no longer a young man and my fragile, hungry body can't keep up with all this. I will have just a bit of rest and then I'll be on my way again, no destination on my mind because I'm so unfamiliar with this New World.

But I need to rest.

Sleep for a bit.

I close my eyes and I wonder if this is all a dream.

A dream...

A nightmare...

The novelist lies in bed, still at the hospital, comatose, but he's not alone. He can't see it but his room is filled with crazies, all waiting for him to wake up, ready to sacrifice him to their fake G-d. The crazies could take him now but they want him to be awake so he can experience the horror.

When the creature enters the room the crazies move aside to make space for it. It moves toward the bed, towards the novelist, and then it looks down, at the last surviving member of a way of life. The creature raises its right hand in the air and then brings it down, its long nails reaching out for the heart of the novelist, a heart that knows all the secrets in Heaven, the difference between good and evil...

"Ah!" I wake up screaming. Famished, too.

I get up slowly from the floor, every bone aching. My brain commands me to move faster but my tired body can't obey the orders that it has been given by the brain.

Before I leave my hiding place I scan the area around me. It is clear but I see smoke coming from far away. Deep in my heart I know where it's coming from. I know what they are burning.

Where can I go now? I wonder.

I'll get my bicycle first and then I'll think of where to go, but when I get to the bicycle someone is already there, going through my notes. I recognise him straight away even though he has aged so much.

"Yu Hua!" I say.

"You remembered it," the former tramp smiles at me.

"Is this a dream?" I ask.

"More like a nightmare if you ask me."

"How long have you been here?"

"I saw you leaving town and I followed you. I didn't want to scare you and I wanted to make sure you were still reliable. Eloise told me what happened and I was ready to kill you, but then I read your notes while you were sleeping, and I knew I could trust you. To be honest with you, I never trusted Julian. Neither of us did."

"Julian? Eloise? Sorry but I'm lost."

"Julian was the man you killed and Eloise was the girl you saw in the lake."

"I'm still lost."

115

"Come with me and I'll tell you more. I'll do better than that; I'll show you."

I do as I'm told and I follow Yu Hua. He left his bicycle not that far from where I slept, and afterwards we ride back to town.

"Are you sure this is a good idea? Going back to town?" I ask.

"We're not going back to town. We're going to a place nearby. And don't worry about the crazies. Nowadays they never stay for too long in the same place. They're looking for something, for someone, maybe for the end."

So we cycle back to town, but halfway there we enter a dense forest and we push our bicycles through the bushes. Yu Hua shares some fruit and cold fish with me. Bread too.

Bread!

A tear rolls down my face when I take the first bite of bread and Yu Hua tells me to eat slowly.

"Everyone is getting used to the New World, to new things too, such as bread," he says as we keep on moving slowly through the forest. We rest by the river where I finish my meal, and after a wash and more rest, we keep on moving.

Yu Hua takes me deep into the forest where others like him, like me; humans, human life, are waiting for us.

I see the girl from the lake, and when she sees me she panics but Yu Hua tells her - and them all - I'm a friend, a man with knowledge, and I mean them no harm.

"This is my little group, our little tribe," he says.

Apart from Yu Hua and the young girl, there are eight more people in the group, the *little tribe* as he calls them; four men and four women. One of the men is Chinese, his name is Ha, and he looks to be in his early twenties, and two of the women are black, from African parentage. I know this because Yu Hua tells me so later on.

"Those women looked after Eloise after her mother died," says Yu Hua. He tells me how he met them all throughout his journey. Some of those strangers were alone, scared and hungry too, but the former tramp helped them and kept them all together. Throughout the years the group kept on growing and moving forward, always forward, in search of a place they could call home.

"Now we live here, in the caves, and we grow our food, catch our fish, and hunt for meat. We intend to stay here for a long time, and with time our group will grow and so will Mankind," he says.

Everyone is listening to him. "Eloise is pregnant. Ha is the father of her baby. So, as you can see, our group is already growing," says Yu Hua. "This is not the end. This is a new beginning."

We hear the distant sound of the car engines. The crazies are moving on, in search of me, searching for something to destroy, but their search will be in vain, and sooner or later they will either die or kill themselves with their hate.

"But what about me? What will I do here?" I ask.

"Teach them. Teach us. Teach us what you know. Write about it so that the Word won't be forgotten. What's the point of having a New World without the Word to guide us?" he says.

I nod.

Yu Hua is right.

What's the point of starting again if we don't know the difference between right and wrong? I must be like Moses and Abraham and teach my people how to live righteously.

And so I finish this diary now. I might return to it later on but I doubt it. Another book awaits me, one that has been written before by my people, but I need to write it again so that my new people won't forget the word.

And the word is love.

Shalom.

UNDERGROUND

A window was left open for a long period of time, and, somehow, our love managed to slip away. Fearing being left alone, like her old friends, Kara tries to please me most of the time, not realising that I want to be left alone. She also wants me to pray but I don't believe in what she believes. She brings me herbal tea when she knows that I drink coffee, but her religion forbids caffeine. Our kids left home three or four years ago. Our son David moved in with his girlfriend and our son Peter moved in with some friends. They both drink coffee and David smokes. Double sin, according to Kara. She got our children baptised in her religion, never allowing me to have a say in the matter, but now none of them follow her religion and they can't even bear to hear her talk about it. Neither can I. But maybe she's right, and maybe we're wrong. And when I think about it, her religion only teaches good things.

I'm up early in the morning and I decide to go to the café just so I can have a moment of peace. Kara comes running after me and asks where I'm going.

"Don't worry. I'll return," I say before exiting the house.

She watches me through the window as I make my way down the road. A jogger running on the opposite direction almost bumps into me and then shouts, "Watch it, old timer."

"You watch it, you fool," I say.

The jogger stops, turns around, and makes his way towards me. I see him grinning, expecting an easy time, expecting nothing from an old timer like me. A couple passing by stop on their tracks to witness it all.

The jogger asks, "What did you call me?"

"I called you a fool."

"How dare you call me a fool?"

"How dare you call me an old timer?"

He shakes his head and laughs, and then pokes me on the chest once. He goes at it a second time, but I apply a wristlock on him and he winces like a baby.

"The pavement is for all and not just for you," I say and he cries, "Yes."

A lady around my age smiles at me. Just because we're old it doesn't mean that we don't exist and don't have the right to the pavement too. I'm as old as Steven Seagal; some people even say I look a lot like him, and I can look after myself too.

Near the café the skaters are enjoying the sun, showing off their moves to the public. I never skated but I tried surfing once. I wasn't good at it.

I enter the café and wait patiently for my turn to be served while the guy standing in front of me puffs heavily. He has a book by Sam Lipsyte and a MacBook under his arms, and a copy of The Times, and he's listening to something on his iPhone, and the puffing goes on and on for a long time, louder each time he lets the air out of his mouth. And then, when is his turn to be served, he orders his ice coffee loudly, the damn music still playing on, and he hands the money over abruptly, never says please or thank you, and afterwards carries his drink and all his shit to a table at a far end of the café, and he sits his big ass on the sofa, not on a chair, and turns the MacBook on, the music still playing loudly on his iPhone, and he browses through the newspaper while typing something on his MacBook, and he takes a sip of his drink and opens the book randomly, and now he has the MacBook on, the music playing on his iPhone, The Times left open in front of him, same as *The Fun Parts*, the book he's trying to read. This man doesn't enjoy life. He can't enjoy it. How can he when he's trying to do a dozen things at the same time?

I'm re-reading Camus. My son lent me a book called *NW* but I couldn't get into it. I've started to go through all the French authors of my childhood; Camus, Zola, Sartre, Genet. My wife doesn't read fiction. Throughout all the decades we've been together all she has read are books by former Presidents of her church.

"Fiction at its worst," I once said to her and she stopped talking to me for a while. Good days they were.

On the way out I buy two coffees; one for the tramp and one for the street writer. The street writer sits outside on an old wooden box and he writes poems and stories for people passing by. I've known him since the day he was born and he has always been a strange person; weird but harmless. He lived in Portugal for a few years, Paris, too, and he has always enjoyed writing but never made a life out of it.

His name is Yasha and his parents died two years ago. They left him a good inheritance and since he lives a modest life he doesn't bother with work. Instead he does this (and this is his work); he writes street poems or little stories, or whatever comes to his head, and every morning he sits here, rain or shine; under a stand if it's raining, and he does his job. Some days he's quite busy and earns well but he also has a lot of quiet days in between. I once asked him what he writes about and he said, "I write what I see, even in my dreams."

"And what do you see?" I asked.

"Everything," he said, "and nothing."

"That's a lot," I said and afterwards I gave him 10 dollars and he wrote something for me.

A man on the edge of a nervous breakdown.
Smoking and thinking; Is this it?
Is this my life from now onwards?
This empty vacuum?
This foolishness?
Me, here, a man in pursuit of an ideal, of a dream, surrounded by idiots;
Is this my life?
The rest of my life?

A man on the edge...

He smokes and smokes and smokes, endlessly, as if the world is coming to an end.
Furiously sucking on the butt, as if he's taking revenge on it for his failures.
For the end of his dreams?
What dreams?
Puffing and scratching his head.
Twisting his mouth, and puffing, puffing.
Puffing his life away.

He's not a bad man.
A man on the edge...
He fights for an ideal.
Never was (a bad man) and never will be.

But his ideal is dead.
Dead and buried long time ago.
Buried alongside the dreams of the brave ones and the tears of the innocent.

He puffs and thinks;
How will I win this never ending battle?
But the battle he fights is within himself.

"Do you write a different poem to everyone or do you sometimes repeat yourself?" I asked and he looked at me sadly.
And then he said, "Sometimes I repeat myself."

I hand the coffee over to Yasha and he thanks me for it. And afterwards he writes a poem for me. Or something.

I read it quickly. I thank him for it and he thanks me for the coffee.

As I'm about to leave, a bored looking woman, red-haired, long legs, approaches Yasha and asks him to write a poem about mermaids. He goes at it straight away and minutes after she had asked him for the poem he hands it over to her. She reads it and smiles, and they talk about something, but I'm already on my way and fail to hear what they talk about.

A fish lost at sea.
A mermaid.
Her eyes blue, a deep blue.
Her hair red, a fiery red.
Her voice the sweetest voice ever heard.
It led men to perdition, to insanity, and drove women insane with jealousy.

A fish lost at sea.
A mermaid.
Where's my hook?

The tramp has no home. That's why he's a tramp. From what he told me, he's been living on the streets for quite a long time. Like you and I – like all of us - he, too, had a father and a mother, but his parents were monsters, and after years of being abused he ran away from home and never looked back. His parents never bothered to look for him and now the streets are his home and he tells me that here – on the street - no one really harms him. He's a young man, younger than my sons, and he has so much innocence and fear in his eyes. He's a victim of life, a son of no one now.

"Some people stare at me weirdly and avoid me as if I have the plague, but no one really hurts me so I can't complain," he once said to me.

He lives off the kindness of strangers, washes himself in the river or wherever he can, and he has most of his belongings stocked somewhere underground where he lives on his own even though hundreds of people, if not thousands, also live underground. He chooses to stay alone because he's scared of his fellow human being.

"I listen to the voices around me," he says, "and I'll tell you this: get ready because the end is coming."

"How should I get ready?" I ask.

"Build a lair underground, get a weapon if you can, stock up on food and water; canned food and bottled water, of course, and when you hear the rumours, hide. Go underground and stay there until you hear nothing, not a peep. And even after the silence descends upon you, stay still. Stay still for a long time. There will be others, crazier than you and I, who will decide to pop out of their hiding places. When that happens you will hear their screams."

"What happens if I pop out too early?" I ask.

"Maybe nothing will happen or maybe you will be affected by the radiation and your face will change, along with your skin, your eyes, and you will mutate into something else," he says.

"How do you know all this?"

"I hear people talking around me; important men, men of power, men surrounded by other men, some of which are heavily armed, and they talk about the end and what will happen afterwards, and they ignore me because for them I'm nothing."

"Who are these men?"

"Rich men, men of power."

I sit on a bench next to him. Someone I know, a friend of Kara, sees me sitting next to the tramp and says nothing. He's a fool, an ignorant fool, an obnoxious man who thinks too highly of himself. I guess someone has to. At church he prays with others, acts all saintly and goodly, pretends to care, but he doesn't give a damn about anyone but himself. So much for being a man of faith.

After a few minutes of listening to him, I say goodbye to the tramp and I stand up. Before I leave he says, "Prepare yourself."

I nod.

We eat tomato soup, followed by chicken with rice and broccoli, and throughout the meal we don't exchange a single word. I wash the plates and cutlery and put them away while Kara watches the news, and afterwards I sit next to her and I grab the Camus book and leaf through it. But Kara wants to talk. Lately she wants to talk a lot.

"Do you still love me?" she asks and I think about it, but if I really loved her would I have to think about it?

She stares at me anxiously, her heart beating fast as she waits for a reply, and the longer she waits, the scarier it gets; for her, for me; because the longer the wait, the bigger the damage, or the bigger the lie.

"Of course," I say, but she's already up, running along the living room, into the bathroom she goes to let the tears come out, an endless river of tears, and I wonder if she can swim or is she drowning?

That night we make love. Yes, couples our age still make love.

The door is open, not wide open but there's a gap big enough for our cat Katt to sneak out and follow me into the shed. In his mouth he carries a gift.

"Thanks, Katt," I say as he leaves the dead rat by my side.

One night I watch Katt go underground near our house. I lift the drain cover and I peer into the darkness. It stinks down there. I go back to the shed and I grab a torch –and my sword, too, just in case... you never know what's out there...and then I go back and I lift the drain cover again, and I go down, all the way down, underground. And you know what –it's peaceful down there; so peaceful.

Every night I go underground for a couple of hours, to tidy up, to get the place ready. I found empty rooms which I can use to stock up. I got a few padlocks and every night, before I go up, I make sure to lock all my belongings behind me.

Kara asks, "What are you doing down there?"

"Meditating," I reply and then I laugh, and it sounds as if I'm going crazy, which could probably be the case, but I don't care.

I stop shaving and I grow a nice beard. I'm sick of being myself. I want to be someone else. I want to reinvent myself, be an action hero.

I shave the little hair that I have left on my head. Kara doesn't like the changes in me. She thinks I'm going crazy but I never felt better.

I buy a couple of gas masks and I take them underground. I stock up on food. Water too. I even take some of my clothes and books underground.

Kara cries and says, "You're going crazy! What will our neighbours say?"

"Keep your mouth shut about this," I say.

More books. More food. More water. Damn it, even if nothing happens I still think I'll move here.

"What's your name?" I ask.

"I like his name," the tramp says and he shows me the book he's reading; *Chronicle of a Blood Merchant*, by Yu Hua.

"What about you? What's your name?" the tramp asks.

"I don't know," I reply for no reason whatsoever. But if the tramp can have a new name what's to stop me from having one too?

Camus is so depressing that after finishing reading it I skip Sartre and I read one of Kara's books, something called *Not the last Goodbye*, and although the subject of the book is cancer, the story in itself is heart-warming.

I've just realised I haven't stocked up on medicine. Big mistake.

I buy painkillers, vitamin C tablets, vitamin E tablets, vitamin B tablets, alcohol, bandages, vitamin A tablets, vitamin D tablets, milk of magnesium, etc., etc., etc.

Kara cries and says, "You've gone crazy."

I tell her to be quiet because I'm watching *Under Siege*.

After dinner she cries a bit more so I head upstairs, into our bedroom, and I watch *Belly of the Beast*.

The next morning, while Kara goes to church, I head to the café. On the way there I see an old student of mine.

"Sensei, long time no see," he says and I smile, and we talk for a bit, and he tells me about himself, about his family, and I say, "Get ready. The end is coming."

"What?" he asks.

"The end is coming," I say it again.

Two days later, I see him again. This time he's not alone. He introduces me to his wife Lingling and their son Ha.

"I've done as you've told me, sensei. I'm getting ready," he says.

"Good," I say.

Three, four times a week, I see the tramp and we talk about cancer, Dr David Servan-Schreiber, Henry Miller, Paris, laziness, women, Steven Seagal, Japan, Aikido, oil spills, John Travolta, talking babies, bad alien movies, bad aliens, bad movies, aliens, movies, etc., etc., etc., and when I get home Kara is watching the news and she says, "Oh, my G-d! They are talking about WW3!"

"Don't worry," I say.

"Don't worry? Don't worry?" She gets up and follows me into the kitchen and watches me put some food into a suitcase, and then asks me where I'm going with the suitcase and I tell her I'm going to stock up, and she starts crying. Damn it, nowadays she cries a lot. Then she talks about her bishop and church, and tells me to go with her and pray, and I tell her to wake up and smell the shit, and I don't even know why I say it but it makes her cry even more, and I'm thinking, "Oh man, do I really want to take her underground with me?"

I call our boys and I say, "Hide! Go underground. Come with me. I have enough food for all."

And they say, "Papa, you've gone crazy."

Cat food.
Katt's food.
I buy tons of it too.
I sell our car and I spend the money on food.
Kara keeps quiet.
Katt meows.

We move out of the house before night falls upon the city. Katt has a huge feast underground. I shouldn't even have bother with food for him as most days he tends to eat out. We go deep, deep underground, and we put the masks on, and we see a greenish fluid in the air. That same day Katt never returns.

We fall asleep with our masks on.

When we take our masks off, and after we eat something, we feel sick and we throw up. Kara panics and she wants to go up and I tell her to wait, but she keeps screaming and says I'm crazy, and I tell her to wait, and she falls in my arms and starts crying, and I tell her to wait.

I'm as calm as a Zen Buddhist monk.

Finally, after days of being underground, I go up and I see emptiness. I pull Kara up and I tell her to remain quiet. Armed with my faithful katana I make my way along the deserted streets, and when Kara calls me Henry I tell her that my name is now Steven.

"Steven?" she asks.

"Yes, Steven." Steven Fucking Seagal (I needed a middle name).

The streets and cars and houses are covered in some greenish liquid, some sticky liquid that runs slowly along the concrete and glass and metal.

What is this?

For a moment I think that I can hear a thousand voices around me, crying and whispering or praying and waiting, and I feel as if this is not the end but a new beginning, and I think that the survivors should take this chance with all their might and realise how lucky they are. But being the wise fox that I am (and paranoid too), I know that not all will be wine and roses, or bonbons and strawberries, or whatever the hell you like, so I make sure to keep the katana close to me.

Kara wants to cry and I tell her to get a grip because this is just the beginning and there's no time to cry, and then she asks me how I can be so cold, and I try to make a joke about it and I say, "Actually, I feel quite hot."

And once the words come out of my mouth she lets out a river of tears, and I hold her close to me, and I tell her to be strong because, as I've said it before, this is just the beginning and we still don't know what's out there so we need to be strong.

"Be strong, woman," I say and she trembles in my arms.

Our house remained more or less just as we left it. Nothing touched, nothing moved. Only the contents in the fridge and freezer have taken a turn for the worse, but there wasn't much in there because I made sure we ate most of it before we went underground. In despair, Kara goes from room to room while I go into the shed to check our stocking. Everything is still nicely stocked: food, water, medicine. Now I wonder what to do with it; shall I bring the stuff that I have underground here or shall I move this stuff underground?

I grab a jar of pickled eggs and I carry them into the kitchen. I lay them on the table and I call out for Kara. And then I wait...

I call for her again...

And then I wait...

A silence as cold as death enters the room I'm in, and, thinking the worst, I make my way up the steps quickly. I knock on the door softly, and then I push it open with the end of my shoe, and I see Kara sitting on the bed, her head down, her little eyes looking at the pictures of our children, our family, our friends, our beloved ones, most of them gone, maybe all of them gone. I sit next to her and I bring her close to me.

We go underground because there are some crazies out there, people behaving violently, being led by some strange creature. Maybe the creature was one of those who came out of its hiding place too soon and got affected by what was in the air, and then mutated into whatever it is now. Or maybe the creature is the evil one, the one who will come after the apocalypse, after (or is it before?) the rapture. Whoever or whatever it is, I'm not going to stay behind to find out.

I saw someone else today, some guy who said he was Elias Piëch, the famous Jewish novelist, a writer whose works I've enjoyed throughout the years. When I first saw him I thought he was someone else, maybe a saviour, but he turned out to be just a fool, I think. I saved his ass, if only temporarily, and then I told him to run because the creature and the crazies were coming for him, and the poor fool wanted to come with me but there's no way I could look after him and Kara.

The crazies and the creature have moved on. I think they're looking for the Jewish novelist. They've left behind nothing but destruction and chaos. They've taken cars and drove out of here like possessed demons. And possessed is what they are; possessed by evil, driven by evil, and their ending will be a painful one.

Once the coast is clear Kara and I move back into our house. And afterwards, while she stays inside for most of the time, I go out for little patrols around the city. In one of those patrols I see Yasha's typewriter, a poem left in it, something about a virgin poet, and once I read the poem I carry the typewriter home with me.

With time, probably due to boredom or maybe fear of being alone, Kara joins me in my travels, and on our first trip together in the New World we go to our children's houses. First we go to Peter's house, which is only a couple of blocks away from us. I've been here before after the apocalypse and told her there was nothing; by nothing I meant no one, but Kara wanted to see it with her own eyes, and afterwards, on the same day, we go to David's house, where I've also been before on my own, and, again, nothing, no one.

Surprisingly, Kara takes it all better than I expected. Maybe she's getting used to the pain, to the loss. I know that I'm not, but I have to act strong —and a bit insane- to keep us both together. If I show weakness then Kara will show weakness too, and what will we do then? We will collapse and die. I. You. Us.

We never leave the city, and we never see another human being although we see other sorts of life; butterflies, rabbits, bees, squirrels, fish. I start hunting and fishing, and I catch rabbits and fish. I cook it all because Kara doesn't seem to have the strength to do a thing apart from reading. She goes through all my books, books that she never touched before, and she reads Proust, Zola, Balzac, skips Camus and Sartre, and then she reads Sam Savage, Roberto Bolaño, Kenzaburo Oe, Rimbaud, and then one night I hear banging on the typewriter and I get up and check what she's doing, and she's sitting at a table by the window, a table that wasn't there before so she must have moved it recently, and Yasha's typewriter is there too, and I ask her what she's doing, and she tells me she's writing, and I ask her if it can't wait until the morning and she says no, and I tell her that I'm trying to sleep, and she says, "Sleep downstairs," and this she says in a sternly manner, without taking her eyes off the sheet of paper, ignoring me as if I'm not even there, and I do as she says and sleep downstairs, on the sofa, away from her and her damned typewriter.

When I get up she's sleeping, and after boiling some water on a little fire I go upstairs, into our room, and I read what she wrote.

My mother used to walk me to school, always holding on to my little hand, and she...

I read ten pages; ten pages is what she wrote last night, and it is about her life and her mother and school and a fight, but I never get to read about the fight because she stopped writing just before the fight took place.

On the next night she's at it again; typing, typing, typing, and in the morning, while she sleeps, I read what she wrote on the previous night; twenty pages this time, and I read about a fight she had with some red-haired girl at school, some fat girl called Jeannie who was always giving her grief, and Kara split Jeannie's lips with two punches, and while she was punching Jeannie, she felt so good, and this is a side of Kara that I've never seen.

Throughout the months Kara keeps writing almost every single day, but she always rests on the seventh day. She has made a calendar and counts the days so as to make sure to rest on the seventh day. I read about her first kiss, her first boyfriend, the cocks she sucked; four, including mine, and she writes how every penis tastes the same, and she doesn't like the taste of it but she likes it when a bloke goes down on her, and she writes about me, about my temper, how she fell in love with me, how she thought about betraying me a couple of times (but she never did), and she writes about fear and loneliness and hope, and one morning I go to read the next entry on her book but there's only one page, not even a full page, only a few lines in it.

I've always loved you, Henry.

I read it ten, fifteen, maybe hundred times, and the tears flow out of my eyes, making everything blurry, but the words are there, engraved in my mind, engraved in my mind, engraved...

I walk towards her, towards our bed, and I see the pills, the medicine, to take away the pain, to make us feel better, and I touch her face, cold now, pale, in rest, so peaceful.

Once I bury Kara I move out of the house. Too many memories in there, too many ghosts, too many ghosts everywhere...

I carry Kara's manuscript with me. She wrote it for me. I was her reader, the first one but maybe not the last one.

I walk for days, for months, for years, stopping here and there, and sometimes I stop for a long time, for months even, and I make myself comfortable in a nice little house, and I fish and hunt, but sooner or later I'm on the move again because the loneliness is too much to bear and if I move on I won't have time to remember.

Little by little, the world is changing again, the sky is getting brighter, the air is getting cleaner, the grass is growing, the world is getting greener, and I witness all these changes, and I know that Mother Earth is happy because there are less of us, less humans that is, and less of us means less pollution, and less pollution means Mother Earth can flourish once again.

But how I miss a human companion, a human smile, an embrace.

How I miss life.

THE TRAMP'S TALE

A petal floats in the river.
A fish floats by its side.
Its belly full of plastic.

A coffee here,
A beer there.
Afterwards, an empty wallet.

I found these poems inside a tent, a tent inside a house, no one in there, either in the house or in the tent, but there were a few graphic novels and poetry books inside the tent, and this too: two little poems, or whatever they are, written on a loose sheet of paper. I took nothing from the house apart from a book called *One Man's Bible* by Gao Xingjian. I read the book in three days. There's nothing to do nowadays apart from reading and search for food. Now that I think about it, that's what I used to do even before the apocalypse.

Food and books; what else do I need?
Company would be good. The last person I spoke to was Elias but he too has moved on.

I cycle past a tobacco shop. I take lighters and matches and tobacco with me. Sweets, too, and gum. Later at night, alone in a house that is now my place of rest, I light a candle and I read a bit more. But then, stricken by fear and scared of the silence, I put the candle out with the tip of my fingers and I listen to nothing at all.
Silence: sometimes it is scarier than loud noises.
In the morning the silence is disturbed by the roaring sounds of cars driving past my hiding place. I peer through the curtains and I see the crazies inside their cars, their shouts almost as loud as the engines of the cars.
After the apocalypse they could have been anyone they chose to be. They chose to be nothing. I chose to be Yu Hua.
They drive by so fast that they fail to see me.
They drive by so fast that they fail to see that the world is changing again and they are being left behind.

131

Hate never survives.

It kills everything in its path, even itself.

I walk alone for days, and the days become months, and the months turn to years, but time has stopped so I'm ageless now and I have all the time in the world, or maybe time is running out and I better hurry up.

But hurry where?

And do what afterwards?

It was a dream. Or so I thought. I was swimming in the lake when two women waved at me. Then they took their clothes off and joined me. I'd never seen a naked woman before. I never had a woman before and I told them so. They smiled and one of them said, "Have us both now."

They laughed and, nervously, I took them both. It was the best feeling I ever had. Afterwards they took me somewhere else, a place not that far from where we were, and there were other survivors in there.

They are dreamers, like me, people who dream of a better world, a place free of hate.

Time is always kind to dreamers.

THE END

I saw a stranger walking by and he stopped where my typewriter was. He didn't look like a writer, but he still took my typewriter with him. Armed with a katana, head shaved, long beard, he looked like an angel of death. Or Keanu Reeves in *47 Ronin*, minus the hair.

Instead of fear and anger, I felt exaltation. (Another human. LIFE!)

I didn't follow the stranger. I grabbed another typewriter, a few ribbons, paper, too (where else would I type?), and I made my way home.

When the end arrived I was hiding underground, doing what the tramp told me, mask on, and I was saying the morning prayers, and afterwards I felt dizzy, and I slept, and I dreamt, and I woke up, and I said the Amidah, the Maariv, and I prayed for salvation, and here I am now, after the apocalypse (not the end), alive and safe, still typing away.

The end arrived and it went away, and it missed me and a few others.

I saw strangers screaming and cursing, chanting songs of hate about my people. I was on the move, searching for others, and instead I saw the crazies being led by some strange creature. They burnt books, the records of my people, the records of the world. They tried to burn History but History never dies.

We are It: History.

We make It.

I saw others, not crazies, but they were fighting over a woman, and one of them got killed, and the woman ran away, and so did I, and the crazies jumped on a ship but they didn't get far. They were hit by something, a missile, I think, a missile that came from a submarine, which means there are others out there, a lot of them, and the ship sank, and the crazies died, including some creature that was their leader. I saw their bodies floating on the water and I kept on moving.

I went back to my city, and on the way there I saw the man that had taken my typewriter. He still had his katana but not the typewriter. He looked older and he didn't see me, which was good.

Maybe he was lonely too, as lonely as I was, but I'm getting used to the loneliness.

I've got so much to write and the world is changing, moving forward, spinning round and round, and the seasons come and go, and there are others out there, like me. I've seen them but I keep my distance.

I like it here.

It is quiet.

It is safe.

It is warm and I'll stay here until my end.

THE FIRST BOOK

Eloise and I found a man, a really old man, and at first, when we saw him, we thought he was sleeping because he looked so peaceful, but then I touched him and he was ice-cold. He had a big sword with him, kind of like a samurai sword, and also a book, a big book, something called *Kara's Life*. We buried the old man along with his sword (because I thought that was the right thing to do; bury the warrior with his weapon), but I took the book to Elias to see what he thought of it.

Elias read a few pages and then he said, "A new Proust."

All of us have read the book and it is really good; a fictional story of a woman and her life throughout the decades, before and after the apocalypse, and Elias told us that the book is very important because it shows that, no matter what, life still goes on and we must have faith.

There are a few rude bits in the book (and I've read those bits plenty of times), and some of the women giggled or looked shocked when they read them.

Elias said, "What a great book this man you found wrote. His *magnum opus*."

A lot of the new generation didn't know what *magnum opus* meant so Elias had to explain it to them.

The book that Elias is writing is also a good one, a book filled with tales of faith and death, and of men and women who were persecuted because of what they believed in, Jewish people like Elias, like all of us because we all follow the principles of Judaism, and Elias said the book isn't really by him. The book is based on the teachings and principles of old rabbis, and every night we read passages of this book, and we also say our prayers throughout the day.

Elias and Yu Hua want us to know the Word, the Word of Good and Evil, and to know the difference between both of them: Good and Evil, and they say we can choose either Good or Evil, but whatever we choose, we will have to live with the consequences of it.

"Choose well," Elias says.

Elias speaks wisely but some of the young lads find him boring and call him an old fool. Some of them talk about rebelling and moving on, away from here, while others talk about death and killing, but who do they want to kill?

This life is nothing.
There's more to life than this.
I would like to tell you more but I'm running out of ink. Maybe next time I...

Printed in Great Britain
by Amazon